Living paintings, spectral children, cannibal serial killers, lost souls, haunted houses, and ancient evil proliferate *The Door and Other Uncanny Tales*. Everywhere reality and fantasy collapse to create a new unstable world, even the body is not what it seems. Combined with Dmetri Kakmi's gothic imagination and mordant humor, the result is fiction that is as memorable as it is unsettling.

This collection contains three new and three previously published stories, including the acclaimed *Haunting Matilda, The Long Lonely Road* and *The Boy by the Gate*.

I0590796

Praise for *The Door*

The Door is a ghost story for modern times—layered, unpredictable and complex. The story goes deep, examining our motives for creating art and exposing the fragilities of the artist in the process. I loved it.

Sofie Laguna, author of *The Choke*

The Door wowed me with the exquisite agony of its characterization and its addictive depiction of very real dread most artists will be familiar with. Absorbing and hypnotic, *The Door* is a great ghost story.

John King, author of *Guy Psycho and the Ziggurat of Shame*

Praise for *The Long Lonely Road*

The power of evocation and suggestion at its best.

Vrasidas Karalis, author of *The Glebe Point Road Blues*

Praise for *The Boy by the Gate*

...a classic ghost story...damned scary and offers up some terrifying images.

IO9 Magazine

Haunting Matilda was shortlisted in the Aurealis Awards, best fantasy novella category.

THE DOOR AND OTHER UNCANNY TALES

Dmetri Kakmi

A NineStar Press Publication

www.ninestarpress.com

The Door and Other Uncanny Tales

Printed in the USA

Print ISBN: 978-1-64890-057-0

First Edition, September, 2020

Also available in eBook, ISBN: 978-1-64890-056-3

WARNING:
This book contains the death of a family member, attempted suicide, prostitution, references to drug use, murder, abortion, domestic abuse, and abuse of a child by a parent.

I'd like to thank the publications that first published Haunting Matilda, The Long Lonely Road and The Boy by the Gate. I am grateful for your support and encouragement. Thanks to Angela Slatter for her work on Light in Her Eyes.

My eternal gratitude goes to NineStar Press's editorial and design team for making me look good.

Foreword

Where do stories come from? I asked myself this question numerous times while putting together this small, representative collection of novellas and short stories. What germ of experience gives rise to a story? The best I can do is to say they come from an unconscious urge inside the author and find sentience on the page.

Often you do not know what you are writing about until someone—a friend, a reader, or a critic—draws your attention to the subject matter. You think you are writing about this, when in reality, you are writing about that. For instance, when my first book *Mother Land* was published a reviewer said the book was about how violence can affect a community like a virus and spread to the most unlikely individuals. "Is it?" I thought. When I looked closely, I saw that on some level it is. I just did not realize it at the time.

The act of violence runs through everything I write. For me it is the ultimate existential question. I am attracted and repelled by it. Why are humans violent and destructive? Why do we treat each other so badly? And what happens to us as moral, ethical beings when we accept violence as a valid option?

The other thing that links these stories is children, often in dire situations. I do not want to psychoanalyze too much, but given my upbringing at a rather volatile time in Greco-Turkish relations, it is perhaps inevitable I keep going back to the locus, trying to understand what happened in the Grimms' fairy tale of my childhood, and why? Each piece of writing brings me closer to and further away from an elusive truth.

Ultimately, I sought to create finely wrought tales that will entrap you in my head for a time, like flies in a spider's web. I hope you are suitably rattled and provoked.

Dmetri Kakmi, January 2020

THE DOOR

For Shane Jones

Chapter One

"There now," Orestes said, standing back to admire the painting.

It hung before him from a sturdy hook on the landing of the staircase leading from the darker downstairs part of the house to the lighter upstairs, with rows of small windows and the French doors that opened on a balcony, overlooking narrow Transom Street. This had been after all, in other times, an industrial area, filled with factories, abattoirs, noise, and the stench of hard labor in the shadow of the nearby Convent of the Good Shepherd, by the river. Now the suburb was gentrified and provided accommodation for the likes of himself, Orestes Gallanos, and his partner Simon Cole, artists both, living the inner-city dream in lofty warehouse spaces.

"There now," Orestes repeated, casting an eye over the artwork he had labored upon for almost five months, in the garage turned studio with its stuffy air and bad light. He folded his arms across a narrow chest, tilted his head to the side, and stepped back to admire the results of his efforts. Not too far back because the hardwood landing was small and he risked falling down the steps to the polished concrete floor below.

It was a splendid work, even if he thought so himself. Very effective. It achieved exactly the outcome he aimed to produce in its creation all along.

It was a door painted with oil on linen. A life-size door, seven feet in height and three feet wide, with an old-fashioned handle that gave off a pleasing brass gleam. The square frosted glass panel above complemented two vertical panels below, and he had found that working with oil allowed him to capture perfectly the desired grain and texture of wood.

He descended the stairs and studied the painting from the entrance hall. From there, should a guest visit, the painting looked like a real door, complete with architrave and wooden step to complete the illusion. Only Orestes knew that, if he should by a miracle manage to open it, there would be nothing on the other side except plasterboard. A guest ascending the stairs and brushing by the painting would assume it was a real door, leading to, presumably, a newly built room on the other side.

At that moment, the front door opened behind Orestes and Simon came in, bringing with him a cold gust of July wind. His hair was cut short and newly dyed blond to accentuate the navy in his deep-set eyes.

"Hello," Simon said, removing the black plastic raincoat and hanging it with a sprinkle of rainwater on the coat rack. "Why are you in the dark?"

It was four-thirty in the afternoon and almost pitch-black in the hallway. Orestes pointed wordlessly at the painting; a smile played on his lips.

"Oh," Simon uttered, coming to stand beside him. "It's terrific. It really is." He gave Orestes a peck on the proffered cheek. "Congratulations. Are you pleased?"

"I think so..." Orestes cupped his chin and stared at his work for a while.

Simon stepped forward, rested both forearms on the staircase handrail, and gazed at the painting with a contented sigh. Orestes bathed in the way Simon was always so genuinely enthusiastic and encouraging about his work. It gave him confidence, made him feel he was worthwhile after all.

The electric light from upstairs streamed down and fell on the painting with intensity, making it resemble a well-lit stage, set for a play.

"Any moment now the door will open," Orestes whispered behind Simon, "and the actors will step forward to pronounce the made-up lines meant for made-up lives."

Simon's smile was warm when he said, "That's what I was thinking." Then he caught the expression on Orestes's face. "Something's bothering you."

"I wondered if I should have the door slightly open."

Simon was also a painter, of a more esoteric order, and, although slightly younger than Orestes, had strong opinions on this sort of thing.

"No," he cried, shaking his head and glancing at the painting as if he might have to fight for its right to remain as it was. "That'd be overemphasizing it. Glass is a kind of opening for one's perceptions even though one's body remains shut out."

Orestes considered. "You're right," he said finally. "Glass lets your eye enter the other side, but only partially, since it's not clear glass."

"Oh, baby," Simon cried, coming up to Orestes and catching his wiry form in his arms. "This can be the centerpiece for a series of trompe l'oeil for your next exhibition. Imagine a whole room!" Simon twirled happily around the floor with Orestes in his arms, smiling and pressing him to his body. The room spun with them, the glass bricks of the bathroom at one end and the darkness of the garage-studio at the other. "This calls for a celebration."

"There's a bottle of Taittinger in the fridge," Orestes offered.

They went upstairs. Orestes popped the champagne bottle and poured the amber liquid in tall crystal flutes inherited from Simon's mother, Orestes's side being poorer and lacking in luxuries and good taste. After watching *Laura* with Gene Tierney for the umpteenth time, they made quiet, habitual love on the couch and much later still, after watching *Farewell, My Lovely* for the sixth time, they crossed to the bedroom and slept soundly in their double bed, behind an elaborate wooden Japanese screen.

In the long winter's night, the building settled with a sigh around them. It resolved its sound angles and determined lines into a world filled with peculiar, shifting disturbances, some fleeting and others lasting, deep in the mortar and concrete of the century-old foundations. The last train raced by unnoticed on the raised tracks a block away, the procession of near-empty windows piercing the night like accusations. In the early hours of the morning, when traffic slowed on nearby Hoddle Street, only the icy wind was left to prowl the empty streets. It slid past the grille pulled over the sturdy front entrance, passed through the barely discernible crack under the door, and set out feelers toward the stairs, from there to reach the painted door with the frosted glass panel and the glistening doorknob. The painting showed faint in the cold silver of a night-light left on halfway down the stairs. If there was anyone at the top of the stairs at that hour, one would have been forgiven for thinking the door looked forlorn on the landing, where people pass but rarely stop. An invitation.

Chapter Two

Early next morning Simon left for a week's stint as artist in residence in Mildura. The couple parted beside the regional train at Southern Cross station, after hugs, kisses, and promises to call every evening directly at six.

"I'll have a glass of red beside me," Simon told Orestes. "You do the same. We can pretend to have our usual drink and catch up on the day's events."

Their ritual for as long as they had been together. Twenty years in August.

Orestes kissed Simon again as the train let off a great blast. It set a deep vibration in his stomach, reminding him of desperate partings in *Brief Encounter,* another of their favorites.

Simon let him go and stepped back into a dusty carriage. Seeing the dirt plastered to the sides of the conveyance brought to mind the great open plains of Orestes's youth and the race courses he haunted as a boy, wishing he were a jockey and looking forward to the day when he would mount a magnificent steed and bring it with skill to the head of a winning race. The image was so vivid in Orestes's mind he almost heard insects creak in the trees; he almost smelled the long, gently bending grass beneath an unending sky. And in that moment his mother turned and looked at him over her shoulder, long springy coils of brown hair spilling down her back.

"See you Saturday afternoon," Orestes murmured with a small wave.

"Try to come up," Simon urged as the automatic doors shut between them.

The train pulled out of the station with a rumble. Simon craned his head and waved from behind a dirt-caked window for as long as he could. Then he imaged Simon took a seat and opened a book for the long journey ahead. No doubt Orestes cut a forlorn figure, standing on the gray, windy platform with an upraised hand and brave little grin on his face. He did not like to be apart from Simon. Separation left a small hole in him, and it grew bigger as days passed, often driving him to despair.

He stood on the platform until the final carriage turned a corner and vanished from sight. Then he retraced his steps to the escalator and ascended to the upper levels. On Collins Street, he mounted a tram and headed to Fitzroy to meet Peter Polites. Aside from being Orestes's oldest friend, Peter was the curator of Sponge Gallery, the space in which Orestes hoped to display a series of paintings. They had known each other since art school, and although Peter was heterosexual they were like brothers, easy and casual with each other. Yet careless, too, the way people who have known each other a long time tend to be, taking it for granted the other will be around no matter what transpires.

Orestes outlined the concept for the show over a cup of coffee as the two hunched beside a De'Longhi electric heater in a small, intimidatingly neat office at the back of the gallery, watching through an open door as Peter's young assistants, a man and woman, dismantled an exhibition.

"Righto," Peter said when Orestes finished speaking. "What do you want to call the exhibition?"

"Fact or Fiction."

Peter was short and stocky, with a beard and rapid-fire delivery. He nodded continually and scratched his bushy chin as Orestes spoke. "And what's the philosophy behind these works? What do you want to say exactly?"

Orestes shrugged; he hated these kinds of questions. "I'm not interested in metaphor or symbolism. So, for me, trompe l'oeil painting can create a state of being where the thing being painted enters the same space as the viewer. Usually with exhibitions it's the other way around. That is, a realist painting has its own space and the viewer enters it."

"So, you're playing with perception."

"And state of mind."

Half of Polites's attention was on his assistants. "Ahmad, be careful with that sculpture and wrap it up properly before putting it in its case." He turned his attention back to Orestes. "I'm afraid that's not going to cut it with the punters. You need a manifesto, a grand gesture that'll make 'em want to part with their hard-earned cash." He tossed back his coffee and looked around for more. When he saw there was none left, he called out to his servant: "Ahmad, get me another double macchiato. Five sugars."

Ahmad, a slender North African with black hair in cornrows, was quick on his feet. "What did your last slave die of?"

"Get outta here, you bugger. Don't forget who's paying your salary. Want another coffee, Orestaki'mou?" When Orestes declined, Peter added, "Why do you paint, mate?"

"Because it makes me feel real."

Peter was horrified to hear this. "Jesus, I feel sorry for you. Most people are into conceptual art nowadays. Painting's dead, they say—"

"Conceptual art isn't real art," Orestes said, sweeping aside the words. "Most of it is crap."

"Crap that sells," Peter said. "Why do you paint, Orestaki'mou? What drives you? That's what I wanna know."

After a moment's consideration, Orestes said, "Much of my work is based on three philosophical questions. Who am I? Where did I come from? Why am I here?" He felt that summed it up perfectly and he was pleased he had been able to gather his thoughts sufficiently under pressure.

"I've no argument with that."

"Since these questions don't have an answer," Orestes continued, "it means we don't know who we really are. We're shut out from ourselves, as if there's a door there and we need to find what's on the other side. It also means we are an illusion to ourselves because lack of knowledge equals illusion."

"What's that got to do with the door you painted?"

Orestes had told Peter about the door earlier.

"The door is a perfect illustration for this condition. The answers to all questions lie beyond the door, if you can open it."

"Sounds better than all those weird beach shacks you painted a couple of years ago."

"They were cabins."

"Yeah, weird cabins, with hooks and blood. Freaked people out and I couldn't sell 'em." Peter stood and clapped Orestes on the shoulder. "Go home and write all this down for me and I'll spruce it up a bit when the time comes. That'll be your manifesto for Fact or Fiction."

Orestes rose to his feet, too, knowing his time was up. Peter was a busy man. Ahmad walked in the door with the coffee, handed the recyclable cup to Peter, and returned to his work. Orestes was walking out of the door when Peter called out behind him.

"How many paintings are you going to do, mate?"

Orestes paused with one foot in and one foot out of the entrance. "About twenty," he considered. "I've already started thinking about two smaller ones."

"That'll do. And Orestaki'mou." Polites approached his friend across the seemingly vast echoing space. "Don't be a stranger. Come and visit. You always go quiet when Simon's away."

Orestes was taken aback. "I do?"

"Don't play innocent with me. You retreat when he's not around. You go into your cave. There's no need. We're here for you." He turned and bellowed across the room. "Aren't we, kids?"

Two timid voices answered in a half-hearted affirmative from across the chalk-white space.

Orestes dropped his voice and said to Peter, "What are you talking about?"

"You obviously forgot what happened last year when Simon went away."

Orestes became defensive. "I wasn't well."

"You know what your problem is?"

"I wasn't aware I had a problem."

"All you Anglos have problems. Bunch of neurotics, that's what you are."

"I'm Greek, in case you hadn't noticed."

"You sold out. You're one of those pseudo-Greeks. That's why you talk with a plum up your arse."

"I see. Please enlighten me. What's my problem, according to you?"

Peter did not have to think about it. "You hold back too much. You should be more... I don't know, open, forthcoming. Grab the bull by the horns."

"Well, thank you for the advice, doctor."

"Well, schmell. Don't be offended." Peter hugged Orestes and added, "Go to your studio and put your neurosis on the canvas."

On the street Orestes turned up his coat collar, dug his hands in his pockets, and turned to take a final glance at the gallery through the large display window. He wished he hadn't. Peter, Ahmad, and the young woman, Alison, stood in a line, staring at him as if they expected him to fall apart on the street. He gave a desultory wave and went his way, not knowing what to think of Polites's outburst.

It was a twenty-minute walk from the gallery to the warehouse in Abbotsford. Orestes decided to risk the chance of further rain and trust to his sturdy legs, although the cold bit through his denim jeans. The air would do him good and allow him to put in several uninterrupted hours in the studio.

Now that it's settled with the gallery, he thought, *I want to start on the work as quickly as possible, while ideas flow and enthusiasm's at its peak.*

Hard work would also fill in the minutes and hours that stretched ahead while Simon was away.

In the end, Orestes worked for four-and-a-half hours straight and came up for air soon after five in the evening. He set aside the paintbrush and cleaned his hands with turpentine before venturing upstairs. The windowless downstairs studio prevented him from observing that it was dark out. The rest of the house was almost entirely sunk in abject gloom. There was not a sound outside. Then he heard it. Soft rain fell on the tin roof and gurgled in drainpipes as it made its way to the gutters on the street.

If nothing else, he thought, *it will give the car a much-needed wash.*

And he slept well to the sound of rain.

It was a short time later, as he sat on the living-room couch, clutching a semi-cold coffee cup in his lap, when the phone rang. It was Simon, of course, and he realized it was already six o'clock. Time for their nightly rendezvous. He put the phone to his ear and leaped to his feet. He headed for the kitchen with renewed energy, switching on lights as he went. The house came to life even as rain lashed the windows.

"Pleasant trip?" Orestes asked, picking up an open bottle of Merlot from the kitchen counter and pouring a liberal helping in a wineglass.

"Long and boring but I got some sleep. How are you?"

"I saw Peter. He's interested in the exhibition."

"That's great. Congratulations. Let's toast to your success. Have you got a glass of something?"

The ritual was ingrained when one or the other was away from home. It bridged distances and brought them together at a time when they least desired to be apart. Feeling slightly foolish, Orestes held up his wineglass, uttered a cheerless "Cheers," and drank. He pictured Simon repeating the same actions in his distant motel room, with the Murray River possibly flowing meters from the door. No doubt it was warmer there than it was in Melbourne.

He turned on the hydronic heaters as he recrossed the floor from kitchen to living room.

"Peter reckons I go underground when you're away," he said, settling on the couch.

There was a barely perceptible hesitation before Simon said, "Do you?"

Immediately, Orestes wished he hadn't said anything. Sometimes his mouth moved faster than his brain. Now that the lights were on inside the house and the heaters busy warming the place, he found his anxiety about being left alone had retreated until it was no more. It was cozy in the house and he liked having the space to himself, even if it was dark and full of shadows downstairs. He looked forward to enjoying a night alone at home. He could watch a DVD, or put in another hour in the studio before turning in. He wasn't answerable. He was a free agent; he could, if he wished, enjoy himself. There was no need to fret.

"Can't say I noticed," he said. "Anyway, it's nice to hear your voice."

"I miss you already. We're in the same state but so far away."

Again, he pictured Simon in the motel room, holding the phone against his cheek and cradling a wineglass protectively to his chest. Was he sitting on the bed or a chair, with bare feet and legs drawn up? What was he wearing? His usual black? And if he was in Mildura, why was his presence so strong in the house? Orestes expected him to come around the corner or up the stairs any minute, smiling and demanding to see a Gene Kelly film so that he could admire the actor's muscular thighs.

They spoke in a meandering fashion about nothing much for perhaps twenty minutes before Simon announced he must get ready for dinner with committee members. He also had to prepare for a local radio interview. They parted after exchanging affections and promising to speak the next day.

"Same time, same place," Simon pronounced, making kissing sounds in the phone.

In the end Orestes fell into bed before ten o'clock and slept soundly, promising himself to get up early next morning and go straight to work in the studio.

He was awoken by the sound of a woman crying. Long, plaintive sobs without end, forlorn in the night. He lay under the warm covers and listened, wondering where it came from. The poor creature. She sounded as if her heart was breaking.

Orestes reached across to the bed stand and pressed the phone's on button. The sleeping alcove behind the Japanese screen lit up briefly; a crazy jumble of shadows leaped on the peaked ceiling and just as quickly fell into obscurity. It was 2.20 a.m. Rain still fell, persistent and driven by wind, in great sheets against the brickwork. And all along there was the woman, wretched and crying fit to break the heart.

When this went on for some time, Orestes threw back the bedcovers and padded hurriedly in bare feet to the bathroom. In order to get there, he had to descend the stairs and walk past the painting of the door, barely visible in the night-light on the landing, as a guide to the second night-light that burned all night in the bathroom.

That's when he realized the crying came from the other side of the wall. He stopped on the landing and put his right ear to the plaster beside the painting. There it was. Definitely. Lengthy weeping and sobbing with no end in sight, as if the woman were alone with no one to take care of her.

Orestes considered the situation while continuing to press his ear to the cool plaster. Robin and Diane lived next door. It didn't sound like Diane. Besides, she wasn't the sobbing type. More like bellowing. Maybe a female friend staying overnight? The two couples enjoyed a close friendship and often had dinner and movie nights where they watched black-and-white films and discussed their merits or otherwise until all hours of the night.

Orestes had a good mind to knock on the wall and tell them to keep down the noise when the crying stopped as suddenly as it started. He stood on the landing, growing colder by the minute in his black boxers and white T-shirt, waiting for it to start again. Nothing happened. There was only the sound of the wind on the street and rain falling. Eventually, he went to the toilet, washed his hands and face, and made his way to bed.

Sleep did not come. He was still awake when the day's first bird sang at six o'clock. For some reason, the weeping had disturbed him and he couldn't get it out of his mind. A tremulous feeling stirred inside him and turned over, like a restless, insinuating beast.

Chapter Three

After breakfast Orestes started work on a new painting without knowing exactly where it was headed. All he knew was that it was to be a full-length nude self-portrait. To make things comfortable for himself, he heated the studio with three small bar heaters, placed a full-length mirror to the right of the canvas so that he could see himself as he painted, and then stripped.

At first it was odd to see his naked body reflected in the glass, paintbrush in hand, eyes moving from mirror to canvas and back again, but then he got used to it. He was so pale and starkly exposed in the familiar surroundings of the studio with its accumulated bits and bobs leaning against walls. His stomach bulged slightly and he sucked it in, promising himself to cut out carbs. He was almost an alien presence in that environment, undressed, out of place and inappropriate. Initially, he concentrated on getting the head right. But his eyes kept straying lower down to the lean trunk, the short white legs, the heavy penis and testicles hanging low between his legs.

For a Greek there was little hair on him. Even less body fat. *Not bad for a man my age*, he thought. Yet he hated to be undressed in front of others. Even Simon. He could not have done it if Simon were in the house. Orestes would have been self-conscious, afraid of being seen and judged. Now he was alone he was free to do as he liked, without fear of being caught or interrupted as he scrutinized his middle-aged body. Oddly, it didn't bother him that strangers would stand before the finished work when it was exhibited. It wouldn't be him then; it would be someone else. He would be an artist interrogating his *soma*, his body, as Greeks put it, and trying to make sense of the age-old question *Who am I? Where am I going?*

Orestes had worked in fits and starts for perhaps two hours when there was a knock at the front door. He hated impromptu guests. Irritated, he pulled on a dressing gown, tied the cord at his waist, and went to see who it was.

"Did I get you out of bed?" Peter Polites said when Orestes opened the door. The gallery owner checked his watch. "Nope," he added. "This is a civil time to call. You gonna ask me in or what?"

Orestes showed his guest to the warm studio and offered coffee.

"Don't want to interrupt," Peter said. "On my way to the gallery after a meeting. With a conceptual artist," he added, giving Orestes a meaningful glance. "Dropped in to make sure you're good, that's all."

Orestes was touched and irritated by the concern. "I'm not going to fall apart just because Simon's away, you know."

"It's called being a friend, mate. Show some gratitude."

Desperate to change the subject, Orestes said, "I started a new painting."

He normally did not show work in progress. Someone always said the wrong thing and threw him off track. But he was desperate to divert his friend's attention away from his perceived weaknesses, and the embryonic likeness was as good a diversion as any.

Peter spun on the heel of his polished black boots and faced the full-size canvas, black gloved hands behind his back. "What's it gonna be?" he said, taking in the outline of head and shoulders.

"Me," Orestes said, trying to make light of it, "in all my naked glory."

Peter nodded but did not say anything, his round head tilted to one side as he contemplated the deft strokes that delineated the beginnings of a human likeness.

"Will it go with the theme of doorways, portals, and all the stuff we talked about yesterday?"

Orestes did not know how to answer; the painting was still taking form in his mind and he could not foresee the end result. Though an idea was worming its way to the fore. When executed it would hopefully give the painting the parameters it needed to fit in with the overall schema of the exhibition. Rather than answer Peter's question, he said, "It'll win a prize. Wait and see."

"I like your confidence."

"It's about time the spotlight trained on my work for once."

Peter faced him, head still tilted to one side. "Are you jealous of Simon?"

"I'm just saying, it would be nice if my work got some attention. That's all."

Peter nodded, unconvinced. "You know the difference between you and Simon?"

Orestes shook his head, wishing Peter would go away.

"He's ruthless when it comes to work."

"I'm not?"

Peter shrugged. "You're cut from a different cloth."

He left soon after, leaving Orestes to stand in his dressing gown in the middle of a studio grown suddenly colder. He shivered and turned away from the painting, the urge to work gone from him for the day. There was no point. Whatever he did would be rejected or at best roundly ignored. He made his way upstairs, turned on the heaters, dressed in black wool pants and a thick turtleneck jumper, and sat in front of the television to watch an old British film called *The Phantom Light*.

That's where he was when the phone rang at six that evening, staring at a blank screen, the movie long over. He reached across in a daze and picked up the phone.

"Hello."

"Hi, baby. It's me. Got your glass of wine?"

Orestes snapped out of it. "No. Just raced up from the studio," he lied. "Been working pretty much all day. Let me grab a glass and I'll be back in a sec." He could have taken the phone with him but he needed a moment to pull himself together. When he returned to the sitting room he said, "Cheers. How are you?"

It had been a busy day for Simon. A gallery floor talk about his work was followed by a radio interview, and then he was driven to a nearby campus to speak to a group of art students. Meanwhile, no one had even thought to ask about Orestes's work.

"Tonight," Simon finished, "I schmooze with a local hotel owner who wants to buy two paintings."

"Is he cute?"

"No."

"Good. Which paintings?"

Simon told Orestes which two works were under consideration for the hotel lobby, but Orestes did not recall them.

"Good luck," he said, feeling unsettled by the conversation. "I started a new painting today."

Simon asked what it was. Orestes was in the middle of telling him how the self-portrait would make the perfect companion piece to the door if placed opposite each other when Simon broke in.

"Baby, I've got to go. The car's arrived to take me to the hotel. They eat early up here..."

"That's fine. I'd finished anyway."

Simon made kissing noises in the phone and just before hanging up said, "Come to Mildura. It's sunny here. And I really miss you."

Orestes told him he'd think about it and hung up. The silence pressed in on him and a night alone at home stretched ahead. Briefly, he entertained the idea of visiting Diane and Robin next door. In the end, he popped a sleeping tablet and went to bed.

He awoke at precisely 2.20 a.m. to weeping. On and on it went, an endless lament. Who could be in so much misery that she could cry with such abandon? After listening to it for a few minutes, he got out of bed and crossed the apartment dressed in a T-shirt and briefs. He stood freezing at the top of the stairs with his hand on the newel and listened.

In imitation of the previous night's events, the crying came from Diane and Robin's apartment on the other side of the wall. He descended the stairs to the landing, put his ear to the plaster next to the painting, and listened. There was no sound other than crying. No words of comfort or solace. Nothing but a monolithic unloading of grief and loneliness.

A picture of a black room filled floor to ceiling with the sound of crying came to his mind.

He was about to bang on the wall and tell his neighbors to keep it down when an extraordinary thing happened.

There was a sharp click in front of his face and the brass handle on the painting moved. Or rather it jiggled in the rectangular plate that ostensibly held it firmly screwed to the doorframe.

Startled, Orestes stepped away from the wall and stared. He was wide awake now, the cold forgotten. His heart beat so fast he felt the thrum of it in his ears.

It happened again. The brass handle moved first to the left and then to the right, as if someone on the other side was turning it.

His mind screamed. *It's impossible. It's not a real door. It's a painted door. Oil on linen. It's not possible for it to move or jiggle or otherwise function as if it was a real door made of wood, with hinges, glass, and brass fittings.*

Yet the handle moved with a slight vexing sound that might have been the wind outside or a tree branch glancing off a glass pane. Abruptly, it stopped.

Orestes was so startled he took two steps back from the painting and bumped his hip sharply against the balustrade. He came to a halt, heart racing, unable to believe the information transmitted by his senses.

Panic threatened to unleash wild horses. But he told himself to stay calm. Take a deep breath and reassess. *It's the middle of the night. You've been woken from sleep under unusual circumstances and you're hallucinating. You think you saw a painted doorknob move. It didn't actually move. You made a mistake. It's understandable, given the poor light and the late hour. Go to the toilet, take one of your anxiety tablets, and return to bed. It's cold. Your hands and feet are freezing.*

The woman's lament had ceased. Silence was complete in the building. Even the painted doorknob remained still as the day he had put the finishing touches to the painting in the studio. He had gone to so much trouble to do right by it, the delicate work required to capture refracted light and a minute reflection in the doorknob of the artist at work on his canvas. It was inspired, of course, by Jan Van Eyck's own reflection in the oval mirror in the painting of "The Arnolfini Marriage". The ultra-fine paintbrush he bought for the job saw to that.

Orestes stood on the landing for another minute, breathing hard through the nose, his hands and feet growing colder than they had a right to be.

The door handle did not move.

The woman did not weep.

Eventually he went to the bathroom, washed his face with cold water, and cursed his contemptible weakness. Why couldn't he be stronger, more resolute?

The question brought to mind a friend's pronouncement from years ago. "When I look at you," the friend had said, "I don't get a sense of a personality. I don't know who you are." Hurt, Orestes dropped him. *One day,* he thought, *I will paint a great painting and then you'll see who I am.*

Chapter Four

He slept late the next morning. After a quick coffee and buttered toast in his dressing gown, he dressed and walked around the corner to Diane and Robin's house. He felt frankly pissed off. Although the adjoining properties backed on each other, the entrance to Robin and Diane's place was on Transom Street, whereas Orestes and Simon's front door opened on Loquat Lane. If Diane and Robin had a distressed friend staying, one of them was bound to be home.

No one answered his persistent knocks. They were probably at work. In the end, Orestes decided to wait until the evening. Despite reservations about going home, he returned and paced from room to room. Upstairs, downstairs. All was emptiness. Only rain and wind to keep him company. People always went away and he was left alone. Abandoned and left to feel unsafe. He thanked providence for Simon. This barrenness, this bleakness, is what Simon kept at bay by the mere fact of his presence. Orestes would face it every day of his life if he were truly alone, with no one to wait for him or care what he did. He couldn't stand it. He'd probably slide and vanish altogether.

In the end, he filled the hours by sitting pensively in rooms carved with a silence that waited in fruit bowls and vases, self-contained and watchful, and on narrow shelves loaded with useless portraits and empty landscapes, all scrutinizing the empty rooms with ruthless, evasive eyes.

A voice in the back of his mind told him to go to the studio and paint. But, for the life of him, he couldn't think of a single reason why he ought. Who cared whether Orestes Gallanos painted or not? No one, that's who. They cared about Simon Cole but not about Orestes Gallanos, the orphaned ethnic who thought he could make a life in the arts.

He only wanted to sit and do nothing. Over time, the walls thinned and finally melted altogether, offering no protection from the outside world. The streets came through brick and mortar and entered the house, full now of previously unheard voices.

When he awoke on the couch, coffee cup draining its contents on the floor, he thought he might have dreamed of his mother and the Benalla farmhouse, under the open sky he had not seen since boyhood.

When he rose and walked in a daze across the living room, it seemed the floor was made of glass. He could see down into the studio where he ought to be, painting for the exhibition, but unable to rouse the least enthusiasm for it. He had nothing to say and lacked even the desire for life.

It was almost five-thirty. Robin and Diane might be home by now. He descended the stairs and went out of the front entrance to see about the woman who kept him awake all night and ruined his concentration in the day.

Diane Driscoll was a tall, well-built woman of sixty. She had a sharp, pointy nose and often joked she should play the Wicked Witch of the West on stage, instead of making a living as a general practitioner.

"What are you talking about?" she said to Orestes, peering around the door and screwing up her small black eyes. She beckoned Orestes in and shut the door against the cold.

Orestes explained about the crying in the night.

Diane shook her head. "There's no woman here. Except for me, of course. Did you maybe...you know..." She smiled and made tippling motions with her hand.

Orestes laughed nervously. "Only one glass when Simon called. That's not enough to make me hear voices." He didn't mention that his eyes also played tricks on him.

"Don't let it worry you," Diane offered. "You can't avoid noise in these high-density areas."

Orestes nodded. "Of course. It's just that it was a strange sort of crying." He shrugged. "Upsetting somehow."

Diane nodded sympathetically, obviously at a loss what to say. Then she asked Orestes if he'd like a drink. He turned down the offer, using Simon as an excuse.

"Come for dinner," Diane said as Orestes turned to leave. "Robin is going to cook a chicken casserole. If he ever gets home." She frowned and checked the watch on her wrist.

Simon's call came through minutes after Orestes walked in the house and traipsed without seeing it past the painting of the door on the landing. He had developed an aversion to it since the previous night's events. On second thoughts, aversion was too strong a word. Perhaps "reluctance" summed it better. A wavering, vacillating trepidation he did not want to transmit to Simon as they spoke.

"Truth is," Simon summed up, "I don't like public speaking. It doesn't come naturally to me. You on the other hand..."

"I attended Toastmasters for two years before I could stand in front of an audience," Orestes supplied, remembering the trembling that beset him and the anxiety attacks.

"Which proves my point. We're painters, not public speakers. I don't see why I should have to speak as well as paint."

"It comes with the territory when you've reached a level of success. Let's face it, you have."

Simon let off a deep sigh. "I know. I don't mean to sound ungrateful." Orestes heard him gulp his wine at the other end and then continue. "A painter hopes the painting will speak for him."

"Unfortunately, that's not how it works anymore. People aren't content to just look. They want to be told what they're looking at."

Simon laughed. "What are you looking at right now?"

Orestes sipped his wine and said, "My reflection in the TV screen."

"A modern-day Narcissus."

"You don't know what you're missing."

"I bet I do," Simon purred. "I miss not sleeping beside you. It's a cold, cold bed up here."

"You'll be back on Saturday," Orestes said, staring at his reflection on the TV's blank screen, "and we can cuddle in bed till the cows come home."

"You decided not to come up then?"

Orestes ignored the disappointed tone in Simon's voice.

"Still thinking about it."

"What are you doing tonight?"

"Having dinner with Robin and Diane and then doing an hour's work in the studio."

Under the circumstances, Orestes thought it best to accept Diane's invitation. The company would do him good. Get him out of the house and stimulate the brain nodules. Knowing Diane and Robin, they would make him laugh, and in laughter, they say, lies forgetfulness.

"Give them my love."

"I will."

"Love you."

"You better."

They saluted the air with their glasses and hung up.

The chicken and button mushroom casserole and lively conversation with the neighbors proved to be a stimulus. After lavish dining and excessive drinking, Orestes walked the dozen or so steps from door to door, knowing there was no one to whom he could go home. He remained awake, busily working on the naked self-portrait in the studio, until his concentration lapsed soon after one o'clock.

He took to his bed and was awoken promptly at 2.20 a.m. by crying. He lay under the covers for some time, eyes open and staring at the ceiling, breathing evenly and trying not to let his temper flare. *It will stop soon.*

If the woman wasn't staying with Diane and Robin, where was she? Where did the sound come from? Could it reach him through an open window from the flats across the road?

He got out of bed, this time making sure to put on a dressing gown and slippers, and made his way across the semi-dark of the upper floor. The balcony afforded only outcast sounds of air currents prowling a world of rooftops, chimneys, and vague traffic noises from Hoddle Street.

He locked the French doors and came to stand, with one hand on the balustrade, at the top of the stairs. The night-light cast its nacreous glow on the landing and on the lower portion of the painted door. The woman's sobs had not been audible on the balcony but they were very much so inside the house. Orestes descended the stairs with the fingers of his left hand trailing the top of the polished handrail and stopped in front of the painting.

The crying was strongest there. From Diane and Robin's apartment. Orestes placed his right ear to the plaster on the right side of the painting and listened. His heart kept a steady, irregular drumbeat in his ears.

Soft weeping, giving way to convulsive gasps, came through the wall. Again, there came to him a vision of a woman alone in a vast, dark room. No furniture. Only her sitting in utter blackness.

As he listened, he tried to think which room in Diane and Robin's part of the building corresponded with the stairwell in this house and decided it must be the living room. Why would anyone leave a distressed woman alone in a living room? It made no sense.

He realized, as he stood with his ear pressed to the wall, that the sound came more accurately from slightly to the left of his current position. He put one foot forward and stepped sidewise to the left, ear now pressed directly to the frosted glass portion of the linen canvas.

Yes, the sounds came from behind the painting. Almost as if...

As the realization sunk in, he became aware that something moved gently, almost imperceptibly, in the palm of his right hand. With horror he realized what it was. He had inadvertently placed his hand over the doorknob when he pressed his ear to the painting. The doorknob moved, like a sleek pelt, in the palm of his hand as it turned clockwise and then counterclockwise.

Orestes leaped back as though he had touched a spider. In that split second he saw the doorknob turn gleamingly once to the right before he bumped his hip hard against the landing newel behind him. The pain was jarring. He sucked in air between his teeth, stopped and stared with disbelieving eyes. From where he stood, he was a mere three or four feet from the painting. His eyes had adjusted and he could see fairly clearly in the semi-dark.

Directly opposite, the doorknob shone brightly in the faint glow from the night-light. As he watched, alternately fascinated and horrified, the handle turned counterclockwise with a slight sticking sound, as though the machinery inside the door needed oiling. A four-pronged star broke on the painted matt surface—he knew it was matt because he had painted it with his own hands—and then dissipated as the handle stopped its circular progress altogether.

Orestes's mind raced. This could not be happening. Yet it was. He was not asleep. He was awake. His freezing toes and fingertips attested to the fact, as did the breath that came harshly from his throat.

Yet it was over now. Whatever phenomenon had taken place had come to a close. It was over. Even the woman had stopped sniveling, like she had at this point in the narrative last night and the night before that. He could go back to bed and he would be sure to confront Robin or Diane the following morning. But why would his friends lie to him, and how come Orestes hadn't seen another person when he dined there earlier?

In a flash he saw himself calling Simon to tell him all about it. But no. Simon would only worry and what could he do about it from Mildura, anyway? In any case, off to bed. First a drink of water to calm his nerves.

That's when he saw the eye. It studied him fixedly through the keyhole in the painted door. The black pupil, the green cornea. The curved eyelashes that trembled as the unblinking gaze locked on him. The alarming vision was blindingly clear to him as he stood with his back pressed hard to the newel post, his hip throbbing with renewed pain.

Orestes was flooded with the appalling realization. Someone on the other side of the door looked at him. Someone who desired to come through and had already tried the handle. Thankfully, it seemed the door was locked. Access could not be gained.

Orestes leaned forward to get a better view. The eye that shocked and appalled with its unwavering truthfulness came by degrees closer. In the convex doorknob inches above the keyhole he saw his own distorted face reflected back at him, together with the suggestion of stairs rising behind. He looked ghastly, pale and spooked, mouth and eyes pulled in different directions, and just when he thought things couldn't get worse, they did.

The eye withdrew from the keyhole and, almost instantly, a face appeared in the frosted glass above.

This time Orestes yelled and, in the process of scrambling back, lost his footing and toppled down the stairs. He slid on his left side the length of the seven wooden steps and knocked his head hard on the concrete floor.

Chapter Five

The air filled with light and warmth, as if someone had switched on a bank of lights and turned up hidden heaters. He stood up and walked to the perimeter fence in front of him. The rambling farmhouse with many windows and deep verandas wrapped right around stood against a cloudless sky, white against the brown fields that stretched for miles in all directions. Sun glanced off the rusted roof. The crab apple tree to the right of the front door was dead and the windmill at the back of the house was motionless and noiseless for once, instead of squeaking interminably as it turned in the gales that powered through the valley of his childhood.

There was not a breath of wind. Still and quiet, except for insects in the long grass by the falling-down fence. A crow in the distance, with its mournful cries. The old-fashioned galvanized steel pipe gate—as umber as the landscape—was hot when he touched it, rust flaking on his fingers. Without taking his eyes from the house, Orestes pushed open the gate, passed through, and stopped just inside, the hinges groaning in the vast silence, setting off an echo he was sure could be heard for miles.

There was every indication that no one had lived there in a long time. The property might even be abandoned. He was thinking this when the front door opened and his mother stepped out. She wore a black house dress with a swirl of white and purple flowers, bare arms, brown hair loose around her shoulders. She stepped forward and shaded her eyes with her right hand as she squinted at him across the yard.

"Orestes," she called. "Come in."

He stood there and didn't say a word, suddenly aware he wore only a dressing gown and slippers.

"We haven't seen you in ages," she called again.

But she didn't venture past the verandah that afforded her a protective cloak from which she dare not break away.

The house stood on a forest of wooden stilts, jutting out of the cracked earth and supporting the underside. From where Orestes stood he saw under it and across the property to the distant mountain ranges.

He thought he saw something stir under the floorboards, a darker shade of purple in the deeper shadows beneath the master bedroom. It crouched on sturdy haunches and waited.

Unaware of its presence, his mother ventured forth and put her left foot down on the first of five steps leading to the ground.

"You've grown," she said, her hand dropping to her side. "A real man."

He smiled but for some reason he could not move. If anything, a greater force pulled him back, away from the house. He had to stand his ground and fight against it, almost leaning forward against its inevitable force.

His father suddenly appeared in the doorway behind his mother. Short and solid as a bull, the man passed through her as if she were smoke and charged across the yard, head down, arms and legs pumping. At first Orestes thought his father was coming for him, but the man passed right by his son as if he didn't see him and kept going at the same pace along the dusty road on the other side of the fence.

Orestes looked at his mother.

"Have a cup of tea," she said. "Before you leave."

Was she aware that the shade beneath the house had come forward and enclosed a strong hand around her ankle? The fingers lay like a sooty ornament at the point where foot connected to leg, anchoring her to the spot.

Orestes looked from her to his father's retreating back and, in that moment, he made up his mind. He would follow the father, closing his ears to his mother's cries.

"Don't leave me alone. One day you'll be alone too... You will be alone. *Alone.*"

Orestes closed his eyes and kept walking.

"Don't forget me."

The road was familiar. He knew every twist and turn, every stone and pebble. There was no traffic and he wouldn't bump into anything unexpected. Waves of sound beat against his ears. His father's shuffling feet, raising dust Orestes could not see, and full of furious purpose in the huffing of his breath. Orestes could smell him and, with his eyes still closed, he followed the familiar scent of tangy aftershave and heavy sweat until he couldn't smell it anymore.

He opened his eyes and there was nothing. Only an empty road.

Chapter Six

"The patient wakes," Diane said from a chair placed at a discreet distance from the bedside. She wore black jeans rolled up at the ankle and a stiff white shirt, open at the neck. A black sensible shoe jiggled at the end of one foot.

Orestes was in bed. He turned his head on the pillow and looked at her. "What are you doing here?"

"You gave me a key to your house, remember?"

Orestes remembered. It happened over a year ago, when Simon locked himself out and had to wait for Orestes to come home.

"What happened?" Orestes asked.

"You tell me. Robin heard yelling in the night. I investigated and found you unconscious on the floor. You've been out for hours."

Orestes closed his eyes against the early morning light spilling through a high window to the left of the bed. It exacerbated the pain in his head and made it throb as if a creature lived in his skull. The long, lonely road lingered, as did the smell of his father's aftershave.

"I don't know what happened. I must have slipped on the stairs and taken a tumble."

Diane looked at him with eyes that assessed each word and found it wanting. Her painted lips were tight when she said, "It's a good thing I have a spare key. Otherwise you'd still be lying on the cold floor."

Orestes couldn't argue with that. Nor could he find a reason to dissuade Diane when she rose and said she'd fetch Orestes a cup of tea, sugary and milky, the way he took it. The only thing Orestes was certain about in his mind was that he could not tell Diane, or anyone else for that matter, the circumstances under which he had taken a fall last night. They would think he was mad or making things up to bring Simon back from one of the many trips he took to promote his work. While Orestes languished at home, forgotten.

The kitchen was on the other side of the wooden screen that shielded bedroom from living quarters. Diane's reassuring voice drifted through the flimsy barrier as she brought water to the boil and proceeded to make tea.

"You're not concussed," she said. "But you shouldn't be alone. Is there anyone who can sit with you?"

Orestes told her there was not.

"What about Peter?"

"He's busy."

"I'll call Simon and tell him what happened."

Orestes sat bolt upright in bed. "Don't do that."

Diane appeared with two cups of tea on a lacquered tray. "He'd want to know."

Orestes lowered his head on the pillow. "He's up there for another three days. Let him enjoy it."

Diane set a lightly steaming new bone china cup on the bedside table and said rather tightly, "You know best."

"He'd only worry," Orestes concluded, catching Diane's tone. "Besides, it's not as if he can do anything about it. Leave it with me. I'll tell him when he calls tonight."

"I can't stay all day." Diane stole a glance at her watch. "I have patients. Everyone's got a cold and they think doctor can make it better."

It was only after she left, promising to visit later in the day, that Orestes allowed his mind to wander back to the previous night. What happened exactly? Now that daylight flooded the room with reason, dispelling shadows, what occurred seemed unreal, fantastic. He could barely credit its veracity. Not to mention his sanity.

A painted door handle can no more move than an unblinking eye can peer through a painted keyhole. *Painted.* The word was important. He clung to it as to a lifeguard. Concentrating his mind on the mundane facts of paint daubed on a surface kept his feet planted firmly on the ground. Rational thought mattered at this point. Otherwise he was afraid he'd float off and be lost.

What then could he make of the figure that appeared behind him at the top of the stairs? It had been a vague outline, impossibly reflected in a painted doorknob. His mind screamed out against it. Yet he was certain the figure had been there, street light slipping into the room to create a sharp contrast behind the form of a woman in a long, loose-fitting dress that fell past the knee.

Surely his mind was making things up, rushing to fill the gaps in retrospect. In truth he hadn't seen so much as a bare outline before the next horror revealed itself. The face in the glass.

Of that one fact he was more certain than ever. There had been a face in the door's frosted glass. The speckled surface distorting and breaking up the man's features yet giving Orestes a clear view that, if he was called upon, he could identify the man in a police lineup.

He could see it now. It had been an uncanny visage. The long neck held in check at the throat with a striped red-and-white T-shirt. The large sensuous mouth. The long bony nose. The set lips. The graying hair that covered the tips of prominent ears either side of a well-formed head. It had been frightfully clear, as though a spotlight had been turned on to afford a perfect view.

Yet perhaps the feature that made the most impression, moments before Orestes fell down the stairs, were the eyes.

The right eye was normally formed, displaying a green pupil that sparked with a hint of light in the white orb. The left eye was appalling. There was no other word for it. Thinking about it pulled Orestes's mouth down at the corners. Perfectly round it was, with no lashes or eyebrows, and located higher on the face than its companion. As if that were not enough, and perhaps to heighten the disturbing effect, the left eye was placed at an abnormal distance from the right. So that, looking directly at it, one had the impression of a lizard gazing to the left of the head.

It was, Orestes thought, the eye of a burn victim. He saw it when he closed his own eyes, as he lay his aching body on the bed.

He was certain of one thing: it was a frightful face, cruel, penetrating, inhuman and untiring. It was in his mind livid as uncooked offal, a dead thing propped up against the glass. It meant him harm. And he could under no circumstances allow it to come through the door.

The dream about his mother and father was nothing compared to that. It only served to remind him he hadn't thought about them in an age. If anything, he'd done everything he could to cut ties and start afresh, leaving the past well behind.

But it seemed the past will not stay in the past.

He was dozing in bed when the phone rang. It was almost two in the afternoon. He picked up when he saw Peter Polites's name flash on the screen.

"Di says you fell," the gallery owner said the minute Orestes put the phone to his ear.

"Diane talks too much."

"Are you all right?"

"I'm fine."

"What happened?"

"Nothing. I slipped."

"Yeah, sure. I know you too well, Orestaki'mou. Something's going on and you're not telling me. But not to worry. I'm not offended. Just to show there's no bad feelings, I've spoken with Simon and he says you're going to Mildura immediately. He misses you. How romantic is that?"

"I have work to do," Orestes objected, tight-lipped. "I can't go running after him whenever he snaps his fingers."

"Listen, mate, your boyfriend wants to see you. Why don't you get your priorities right and go? Your work will be here when you get back."

"Very well," Orestes said, just to get him off his back. "I'll drive up tomorrow morning."

The ruse worked. Peter said, "I'm glad you see sense," and hung up.

Chapter Seven

Orestes didn't mention the conversation with Peter Polites when Simon rang that evening. Simon asked if he was all right, Orestes said he was fine and then Simon said, "Are you coming up?"

"I can't. I've an important appointment tomorrow."

Simon knew better than to push the issue. After that they spoke for some time about the day's events, people Simon met, and what was happening in Mildura that evening at a special dinner. The silence at the other end finally prompted him to say, "Hello, Orestes, are you there?"

"I am."

"You sound distant," Simon replied. "As if you're in a different country."

Orestes supposed Simon was right, as he was in most things. Orestes was withdrawn. Why not? He had a great deal on his mind. Mildura is hundreds of miles away from Melbourne. Possibly that's why he felt removed from Simon. He was so far away. Orestes felt as if he had been placed in a raft and set adrift in stagnant waters, while Simon zipped past in a speedboat. Orestes wanted to throw out a life ring, to make contact, but the impulse collapsed inside him as soon as he thought it. The internal mechanism had shut down and he knew if he so much as opened his mouth without caution and forethought he might say something he'd regret.

He shifted his position in the bed, moved the phone to his right hand, and said, "Sorry, I was thinking of a new painting."

Simon chuckled intimately in his ear. "That'd be right. There's me babbling and you not even listening."

"I said I was sorry."

"I'm teasing." The silky purr lodged an image in Orestes's mind of Simon bringing his lips closer to the phone's mouthpiece. "Tell Mama, tell Mama all," Simon added, quoting Elizabeth Taylor from *A Place in the Sun.*

Orestes couldn't help chuckling. It was their favorite line from one of their favorite films. For a fleeting moment Orestes even saw himself hunched over and holding the phone desperately to his ear, much as Montgomery Clift did in the film as he opens up to the woman he loves but can't have.

"I've been having a bit of a weird time," he confessed. "And just now, when you were speaking, I remembered I had a peculiar dream."

"What kind of dream?"

"About Mom and Dad, actually."

Simon was silent.

"Funny isn't it?" Orestes went on. "People die, we get on with our lives and rarely think about them."

"I don't know," Simon put in. "I think about Myra all the time."

Simon's older sister died two years ago.

"Mom died long ago. She might as well have never existed."

"You know that's the most you've ever said about your past."

Caught unawares, Orestes said, "Is it?"

"Yes. You never talk about your upbringing. I know almost nothing about you before we met."

"Nothing much to tell really. I came into being when I met you."

"Well, I'm glad of that small miracle." Simon sighed at the other end of the phone and it sounded oddly like wind in trees.

Orestes was warmed by the words. "You mean that?"

"Of course, I mean it."

He regretted the words as soon as they came out of his mouth. "Then why are you so far away?"

"Orestes, please let's not go over that again."

"You're right. I'm sorry I mentioned it. Hey, guess what?" he added, hoping to change direction.

He thought Simon was more cautious than he needed to be when he said, "What?"

"I have an idea for a new painting."

"What is it?"

"The reverse of a picture frame."

"Please explain," Simon said, imitating the infamous One Nation leader.

"Normally," Orestes said, "you look at a painting from the front. You see what the artist paints on the canvas. You don't see the back. You don't see what's holding up the painting."

"You mean the frame?"

"The structure or edifice that supports the illusion we admire from the front. We don't see the staples securing the canvas to the wood frame. We don't see the wire to hang up the picture. We don't see any of that. Now imagine a painting, a trompe l'oeil, that presents the viewer with what's normally hidden. If I can pull it off, people will look at it and think it's a real picture frame that's been hung the wrong way."

"A painting that's facing the wall." Simon, too, was swept up.

"A painting that wants to be truly examined."

There was a pause and then Simon said, "What made you think of that, I wonder?"

"Since I look at the backs of canvases lined up against the wall every day, it occurred to me a painting of the inverse of a painting would be very evocative. When you think about it," he added when Simon didn't say anything, "nothing evokes emptiness more than the back of a painting. It's a blank, a void, waiting to be filled. A purely utilitarian and overlooked space. And yet it's so important on a structural level. The painting we admire from the front can't exist if it wasn't for the frame and the wire that holds it up at the back."

Simon breathed audibly through the nose before saying, "It sounds so lonely."

"But so important."

"Like a brassiere," Simon put in. "You can't see it but the effect is swell."

They laughed and then parried like this for a time before the verbal tussock tossed back and forth between them subsided and diminished altogether. It was pleasant to talk with Simon after all he had been through.

He heard Simon sip his wine and cough in a muffled fashion. Then Simon said, "It could be a confronting image to encounter in a gallery."

"I hope so."

"I can't wait to see it."

"You're probably the only one who wants to see it."

"Stop saying things like that."

"It's the truth."

"Just hurry and finish it."

The conversation meandered for a while before Simon announced he must get ready for company.

"Let's toast the new painting before I go," he cried. "Have you got a glass of something?"

"Yes," Orestes lied.

Leaning against the pillows, he pretended to hold up a wineglass in a desultory manner, uttered an automatic "Cheers," and took an imaginary drink. At the other end, Simon smacked his lips, flung a kiss in the phone, and quite suddenly Orestes was left holding to his ear a brick that emitted the emptiness of outer space. He knew he could never truly enjoy anything else again. Yet his heart soared when he thought of going to the studio to begin work on the new painting. The nude could wait.

Chapter Eight

Orestes had been working at a fever pitch in the studio when there came a knock at the front door. He checked his watch. Seven-thirty. It would be dark out. Who could it be? It was Robin, Diane's partner, in a black hooded plastic slicker. The man stood at the door looking for all the world like the Grim Reaper. The rain and wind sweeping in from behind him brought startled musical life to the chimes in the entrance hall, completing the dramatic picture.

"Diane said to check up on you," Robin called above the deluge that poured around him. "She's still at work."

"Come in," Orestes replied.

Robin was of a more reticent nature than his partner. "Don't want to disturb." He proffered a plate covered with a tea towel. "Just wanted to give you this, in case you aren't in the mood to cook."

Orestes took the plate. "You sure you don't want to come in?"

"Call if you need anything." Robin ran off in the saturated gloom.

It was at this point Orestes became aware of the rain that had been falling for most of the day. All along it had been in the background. Now it rushed to the fore so that his mind was almost overwhelmed by nature's force and determination. The street was polished bright, the downpour so strong it leaped off the pavement in dancing spears. The water flowing noisily in gutters and through downpipes created the impression that the world had turned to liquid, on the verge of disintegration. Even the train, when it passed a block away on the raised tracks, was muffled and distant. *Clack-clack, clack-clack*, in the night.

Orestes closed the door and scuttled contentedly to the studio where heaters brought the room to the consistency of warm toast. An overhead light and three strategically placed lamps provided illumination. Behind him, rain beat on the garage roller door and asked to come in. He barely savored Robin's meal before turning his attention to the fifty by fifty centimeter medium density fiberboard. The painting of the reverse of a picture frame was coming along just fine. It was already taking shape as he saw it in all its deceptive perfection in the mind's eye.

He worked well into the night, barely pausing even to visit the bathroom.

When he finally stopped it was 2.00 a.m. The back of his head ached and the eyes were weighty in his skull. He wanted sleep, but tonight was not the night for it. There were more important tasks at hand.

He set aside the brushes he had been using, cleaned his hands on a rag, and turned off all but one light in the studio. The hallway was dark when he stepped into it, his outline falling black at his feet, a guardian animal, as he made his way to the bathroom. The rest of the house, the entire length of the upstairs, was dark and cold. He felt it press on him like a coffin lid. It was a weight that squeezed Orestes into himself, narrowing his options and alerting his senses. He hadn't bothered with the upper floors since the call ended with Simon hours earlier and he came downstairs.

Funny how quickly houses grow raw and unfamiliar when neglected.

In the bathroom, he tidied himself and stood examining his face in the mirror over the hand basin. He leaned forward and stared long and hard in his eyes. There was no sense in what he saw. It was after all merely a collection of molecules that made up skin and bone and hair and blood. The long neck emerging from the red flannel shirt, the high, broad forehead, and large ears covered by hair graying at the temples seemed alien. If he stared long enough into his own eyes he felt sure he would disintegrate—an imperfect illusion that called itself Orestes Gallanos.

Is this who he was? There were days when he felt gossamer thin. A rainfall could break him up. Surely there was a sturdy mast inside him. Something to keep the rigging in place. How to access the real man behind the facade? Might a knife applied to the thin layer of tissue do it?

He left the bathroom, went upstairs, turned on the downlight in the kitchen, and sat at the top of the stairs. From there he had an uninterrupted view of the painting of the door. It stood like a challenge halfway down the stairwell. A challenge and an invitation...

According to his watch it was 2.10. Ten more minutes before the infernal woman started to cry and the whole show began again as though it were caught in a loop.

Seconds passed. It was cold and he wished he had thought to turn on the heaters or to put on a jumper, but he didn't want to move in case he missed the moment it began.

He leaned his head against the baluster, hugged himself to ward off the invading chill, and wiggled his toes inside thick socks and sturdy shoes. His eyes must have closed for a moment because when he opened them again, his heart almost jumped out of his mouth.

The door was ajar. It had been closed. Now it was open. Open outwards to offer a view of an inky interior, and drifting through, like the thready music of a violin, was the woman's lament, eerie and softly tugging at the heartstrings.

At first Orestes was so startled he didn't know what to do. Then he pulled himself together and checked his watch. It was 2.50. He'd slept for forty minutes. Had the door been open all that time?

He stood and with steady steps descended the stairs.

Chapter Nine

When he was nine years old, Orestes came home from school with headache early one day to hear his mother make the most extraordinary noises in the master bedroom. It sounded as if she was in pain and possibly weeping. He was hesitant, yet curious and unable to stop himself as he crept the length of the corridor, bathed at that time of the day with the red and blue glow coming through the lead-light glass either side of the front entrance.

Why was his mother crying? Long, low sounds of exquisite suffering. Gasps. Moans. What ailed her at this time of the day, when Orestes's father was in town and Orestes ought to be in school? Maybe he could offer comfort?

The bedroom door, when he reached it, stood slightly open, offering a glimpse into a sanctum from which he had been banished at the age of five. He only knew that somewhere to the left of the door, in front of the heavily curtained bay window of the Victorian farmhouse, was the expansive bed reserved purely for his mother and father's use and under no circumstances, his father had said, was Orestes to enter once he had been cast out. Yet there he was lifting a trembling right hand to the door, intending to go against paternal orders.

The door drifted open under the smallest pressure from his fingers.

His mother was propped on the bed with her skirt hitched around her waist. Head thrown back, spine arched, and eyes closed, while a man in a red-and-black checked shirt kneeled between her thighs. Both adults were fully dressed and utterly lost to the world. Orestes could not believe his mother's delicate frame could emit such animal yelps, while her legs spasmed and wrapped around the man's strong back, pressing his face further into her deepest self, and, in that moment, her eyes opened.

"Mom?"

The word was barely out of his mouth when the woman flew across the room and delivered a sharp slap to his face.

"Get out," she cried. "And if you say anything to your father, so help me God I'll kill you."

He ran to the backyard, holding his enflamed cheek and failing to hold back the tears that stung his eyes. The red utility van he'd seen earlier in the driveway sped away soon after, leaving a pall of dust in the air, a harbinger of things to come.

Years later, when Orestes revisited this moment in his mind and realized what had happened between his mother and the strange man, the detail that alarmed him most was his mother's eyes. When she saw him standing in the doorway, there had been not a trace of his mother in the two large orbs he thought he knew so well, the eyes he had come to look upon with unfailing love and trust. They were the eyes of a stranger stumbled upon in the dark. It was as if his mother had gone away, leaving behind a woman who neither saw nor cared about Orestes. Sure enough, when she emerged later from her room to go about her daily routine, she talked as normal about this and that, without once looking at her son's searching, perplexed eyes.

Even so she must have seen Orestes nuzzle up to his father later that evening to whisper in his ear about the strange man in his mother's room. She must have known her secret was out. That her son had taken sides and she was, against all expectations, betrayed.

Orestes thought of this incident as he stood on the landing, staring at the door he had created with the aid of brushstrokes and colored pigments on linen. It was slightly ajar, just like his mother's door had been all those years ago.

Should he enter? At what cost? The thoughts shot through his mind as he placed his left hand on the door and pulled it open.

It opened outwards, onto the landing.

The space beyond was sunk in darkness. It was so black in there it made him think that night had been painted over with the old Caran d'Ache ink you couldn't get any more, a void so immense his mind could not comprehend its enormity. It was solid as a brick wall and standing upright before his eyes. He could see nothing past the threshold except sooty black.

"There must be a room in there," he reasoned aloud, "because the woman continues to voice her discontent."

He stepped inside. The ground beneath his feet was solid yet oddly plastic, firm yet soft and yielding. He held the door open with his right hand. He did not want to be imprisoned, come what may.

As he stood for a moment, contemplating his next move, he heard a noise from the kitchen above his head.

There it was again. Footsteps, moving confidently and without hesitation across the floorboards, from bedroom to kitchen.

Orestes's heart almost missed a beat when he realized someone was in the house. Without warning the footsteps stopped and he heard the tap run over the kitchen sink. A glass was filled with water. After a moment, the glass was set soundly on the metal kitchen bench and once more footsteps commenced their movement. Soft, shuffling footsteps, this time toward the stairs.

The intruder was sure to see Orestes if he passed at the top of the stairwell.

Instinctively, Orestes stepped further inside the black and gently closed the door. He did not want to be spotted. More time for Orestes to prepare and somehow disable the intruder.

He applied his face to a corner of the frosted glass in the window and waited.

The shadow that fell across the floorboards at the top of the stairs belonged to a man in a dressing gown and slippers. The bare ankles moved swiftly by and disappeared in the direction of the balcony.

Orestes ought to do something. Alert someone. Bring attention to the burglary.

He put his hand to his shirt pocket and realized he must have left his phone on the coffee table in the living room. Or possibly at the bedside.

The woman's relentless cries continued behind him. It was a miracle the intruder didn't come to investigate.

The thought still lingered in Orestes's mind when the thin legs reappeared at the top of the stairs and, after brief hesitation, began to descend. Carefully, one step at a time. Orestes nimbly stepped to one side of the glass, so that the intruder could not see his face peering through. All the same, he had an uninterrupted view of the man's indistinct outline as he came to a halt in front of the painting.

The intruder stared. After a moment, the man applied his right ear to the wall beside the canvas as if listening for the source of the keening that continued unabated behind Orestes. After a while, the man applied his ear to the canvas.

Afraid the man might attempt to open the door, Orestes grasped the handle from the inside and in the process caused the knob to shift to the right and then to the left. The intruder yelped and leaped back as if he'd been struck a blow to the face.

Although the man had stepped away from the door, Orestes could still make out a fuzzy outline hard up against the baluster. The man seemed to be of average height and of slight build. As he stood in a posture of defensive alarm, Orestes wasn't sure what the man was capable of doing should Orestes step forward and confront him in his own house.

It occurred to Orestes that he ought to get a better look at the intruder for later identification.

He bent forward and applied his right eye to the keyhole beneath the door handle.

The effect on the intruder was almost immediate. His posture stiffened. An expression of sheer horror crossed his face and then, shock replaced by disbelief, he leaned forward for a better view.

Feeling as if he had nothing to lose, Orestes removed his eye from the keyhole and stood up straight to bring his face to the glass. It was a challenge. More than anything he wanted to scare the man. To get a response. To let him know he was not alone. That he was being watched. To frighten him and to show that he, Orestes, was not frightened in his own home. He would triumph.

Thus he presented to the spectator on the other side of the glass a visage of utmost hostility and malice, making sure the contempt he felt for the burglar was focused in the flatness of his eyes.

Much to Orestes's pleasure the man yelped again and leaped back. But his satisfaction was short lived. The intruder collected himself in the instant and then fell angrily on the door, fists pummeling and feet kicking. Muffled shouts and threats came through as, panicked, Orestes retreated.

"Come out of there. Who are you?" sounded distantly in his wake.

As he stepped away, Orestes made out the faint outline of another figure standing atop the stairs, looking down at the man.

At first glance, it looked like a woman in a nightdress. It was only when he continued to study the form that he realized the dress was, in fact, empty. There was no body in it. No head. No arms, no legs. The garment was suspended in air, as though propped up by darkness.

Alarmed, Orestes backed further away, deeper into the gloom. For the time being, at least, he was glad the door held.

There were two people in the house. His own house. They must have come in while he slept. But how was it possible? Had he been so deeply asleep, he hadn't heard them come in through the front door and go up the stairs? They must have walked right past him. But that was absurd.

His mind couldn't encompass the idea that the male intruder had been wearing his own dressing gown and slippers.

How he wished he had never painted the damned picture. He felt sure it was somehow related.

In any case, Orestes was glad they were out there and he was in here. Hopefully, they couldn't come through. After everything that had happened, he couldn't summon the strength to confront them. He must gather his strength and come back. And although he had every confidence that he could describe the man to the police, he also knew a description could only baffle.

It fit down to the last detail his own self perfectly.

Medium height. Slight build. Prominent ears. Long, narrow nose. Graying hair. The pale-blue wool plaid check dressing gown he loved to wear in winter. Even the thin hairy ankles had been recognizably his as they descended the stairs, step by inexorable step.

He felt as if, in the dead of night, he had confronted himself, and, in doing so, uncovered a black hole.

Chapter Ten

Orestes turned from the door and received another shock. The black wall was gone.

He was confronted by a corridor of honey-colored floorboards with a long thin rug down the middle. The deep luster in the boards was flushed with soft light filtering through red-and-blue stained-glass windows either side of a door at the other end. The air smelled faintly of dry flowers, trapped hot air, and furniture polish. The corridor was long and narrow, lined with four doors, two on each side. All were closed. Yet he knew that if he opened the first door to his left, he would uncover a familiar room. His own when he was a boy at the farmhouse in Benalla. A room with a single bed next to the window. A wardrobe, a desk with a wooden chair, and a chest of drawers with an oval mirror. There was little room for the young occupant to sit on the rug and play his solitary games during the stultifying summer days.

The crying, which had subsided, started up again from the end of the corridor. There was no doubt. It was a grown woman sobbing in the depths of her solitary life.

She could wait. He had to check on someone else first.

Orestes pushed open the first door on the left and glanced in the room.

A boy looked up from the desk. He looked to be about ten years old, thick black hair falling over prominent ears. The boy set aside the pencil with which he wrote in a lined notebook, stood from the chair, and came forward with a solemn expression on his face.

Oreste's heart was in his mouth. *Such a serious kid*, he thought. *So small for his age.*

The boy placed a finger to his lips. "Shh," he said. "She mustn't hear."

"Why not?" Orestes whispered, though he knew the answer. He only wanted the boy to continue talking because the familiar voice was an exquisite knife to the heart.

"She's sick," the boy added. "Dad's gone to get the doctor, but he's been gone a long time."

"Have you checked up on her?"

The boy shook his head. "I'm not allowed to go in there. But you are."

"I am?"

The boy nodded. "You're an adult."

He took Orestes by the hand and led him down the corridor.

"Come on, you have to talk to her."

The pitiful sobs intensified as the duo approached the door behind which the imprisoned woman wept. It was almost as if she knew they were coming and wanted to draw them into her imponderable web of pain and agony, and yet, conversely, to repel them. She had played these games all her life. It was come one minute, go the next. And when Orestes finally did leave, he left for good. Never looking back. Yet here he was, trying to make amends.

A part of Orestes hated her for manipulating him. Yet another part, the small, boyish part that held his left hand in a tight grip, slowly drawing him along, felt sorry for the woman and wanted to save her. Or at least to make up for betraying her and ruining her marriage in the process. It was his fault his father left. His mother had said so many times, and he believed it, spending the rest of his life searching for that elusive male figure to make up for the one who left. Who would always leave or betray him.

The man and the boy he had once been stood outside the bedroom door. It was firmly closed and unyielding as a castle keep.

"Go on," the boy whispered, indicating that Orestes open the door.

"No." Orestes shook his head. He remembered all too clearly what had happened the last time he opened a door that should remain closed.

"You have to."

Still clasping Orestes's hand, the boy lifted both their hands and placed them one on top of the other on the brass doorknob. Together they turned the handle and allowed the door to swing open.

The woman hunched on the edge of the bed was pale and shrunken. Her hair almost entirely gone, offering to the world a bald pate with wisps of hair.

There's nothing left of her, Orestes thought.

This is what she looked like after the cancer treatments. So thin that her cream-colored satin nightdress with the elbow-length sleeves had nothing to cling to and hung off the ghost of her frame as a last resort. When she gazed at Orestes, her eyes were flat and dull with resignation. There was as little recognition in them as there had been when Orestes opened the door and found her with another man.

"Need to go to the toilet," she said. "Soiled myself."

Afterwards, having cleaned her and dressed her in fresh clothing (the perfidy of looking on his own mother's naked body, barely daring to touch), Orestes put her to bed and didn't know whether it was himself or the boy who lay down beside her, outside the thin covers, holding her close. She was skin and bone. Gone was the soft, inviting flesh he'd come out of as a baby and joyfully fell into as a boy in need of comfort. Her breath was labored, a frightful wheezing in the chest.

It was only when he thought she was asleep, that he leaned close and whispered, "I love you, Mom."

"I love you too," she said, before resuming the death rattle that saw her out later that day.

The doctor never came. Nor did the husband. After the small funeral, the farm was sold and Orestes lived with his mother's younger brother and his wife, until he ran away at eleven years old.

Now, Orestes awoke on the floor. The bed was gone. The dying woman was gone, taking with her the unnerving breathing, the sickly smell of death and feces. The room was empty and still. Even the boy had disappeared. Orestes lay there for some time, thinking about all that he had seen and heard.

He hadn't thought about his mother in a long time, let alone visited her grave. Is that where he was now? Her grave? Or was he trapped in his memories of her? Inside his own guilt and fear? For all he knew, this was a tomb from which there was no escape.

As for the boy, he didn't exist anymore either, did he? He had grown up and turned into a man, with a life of his own. He, too, was as distant and untouchable as if he had died long ago. In a real sense, neither boy nor man existed. They were memories tugged back into a past more real than the present. Why disturb them now, of all times?

Let sleeping dogs lie, he thought, sitting up.

Except of course the boy had grown up to be a man who refused to commit to anything. A man who stood back from life. Who did not take risks. Who held himself in check, one step removed, too afraid to give and too afraid to take. Neither part of life, nor quite out of it. It was as if he didn't exist. No wonder Peter Polites accused Orestes of holding back. Not giving of himself.

From the floor, Orestes looked at the room. It was medium-sized, with one large window looking out onto a bright sunny garden; he was sure he heard birdsong. Shiny floorboards radiated in neat horizontal lines from where he sat and joined with the skirting boards, painted white, just as he remembered, to form straight walls and a high ceiling overhead. There was not a cobweb or show of dust anywhere.

It was like looking at the room after his mother's brother, Arthur, and his wife, Melissa, emptied the place of furniture and put the farm up for sale.

The walls seemed to shrink in on him and the ceiling to lower.

That's when he heard footsteps in the corridor, light and unobtrusive. Someone out there was trying not to draw attention to himself. The footsteps stopped on the other side of the closed door and Orestes had a sense of someone standing there, listening. A floorboard creaked. The doorknob began to turn.

Orestes's heart tripped wildly in its cage of bone.

"Who's there?" he yelled.

The doorknob stopped turning and footsteps moved rapidly down the corridor. This time they were heavy steps, as if a man in boots ran on bare boards. The echo turned into a kettledrum in his ears, booming until it hurt.

"Stop," he yelled.

The sound stopped. He realized that, while his attention was on the footsteps, the walls had closed around him. He sat in a long, confined space, the walls on either side pressing almost to his shoulders as he looked at the back of a distorted, elongated door. His only escape.

Panicked, before he could be crushed, he crawled on all fours and flung open the door.

The corridor was empty, the light diffuse and melting away. With each step he took toward the boy's closed bedroom door, knowing full well that he was revisiting the day he saw this house for the final time, the awful dread, the appalling realization, spiraled up in his body until his legs felt as if they were weighed down with lead.

He stood in the corridor for a considerable time, not knowing whether to go in or not. In the end, he placed his right hand on the doorknob, turned it, and pushed open the door.

The boy hung by the neck, turning slow, lazy circles from the end of a slender white rope tied to a hook in the ceiling that once held up a mosquito net. A chair lay on its back on the floor at his feet. And as the body turned anti-clockwise, tongue sticking out, head to one side, the skin on the neck stretched, there came to Orestes's ears the sound of the rope creaking as it strained to maintain the albeit slight weight hanging off it.

Orestes gasped with horror, even though he knew in advance what he would find. He also knew that, moments after the boy kicked away the chair, Arthur found his nephew. He had rushed into the room, hefted the boy up by the legs, and called out to his wife to cut the rope. They rushed Orestes to hospital, saving the boy's life with not a moment to spare.

In the years that followed, no one spoke about the note the boy left behind. And then one day, when the boy was eleven, he disappeared from their lives, never to be seen again.

The adult Orestes stood by the boy's desk, reading the words scrawled in a childish hand on a scrap of paper and left on the bedside table when the boy's eyes opened and locked on his. In that gaze he saw a range of emotions: accusation, challenge, fury, fierce determination, and calamitous loss. Most of all it was the horror of realization of what he had done, as the legs started to spasm and the boy's bladder released a flood of urine on the floor.

The odd thing was the body continued to turn in an anti-clockwise fashion, so that one moment Orestes looked directly into a pair of wide-open eyes and at the next moment at the back of a dark head.

Eyes, back of head. Eyes, back of head.

Rope creak, creak, creaking, like a testament.

It was only when the eyes presented themselves for the final time, and Orestes saw they were closed, that a great force shoved him aside and rushed to the boy's aid in the form of Uncle Arthur.

Orestes backed out of the room and found himself staring at the back of the door he had painted on linen and hung from secure fastenings in the wall on the landing of his own home in Abbotsford. Where he lived as a grown man, with his partner Simon Cole.

Simon who was due to return to him in a few days.

How he looked forward to that. But he would not go to Mildura. No, he would make Simon come to him instead.

Orestes touched the scar around his neck. It had faded over the years but it had never gone away. That's why he always wore scarves, turtleneck jumpers, and buttoned-up shirts in public.

He reached out to open the door when he heard his phone ring upstairs. The familiar 1950s sci-fi theremin sound he had programmed into his iPhone. He could tell from the direction of the sound that the phone was on the coffee table in the living room, in front of the television. Through the glass panel, he saw in a blurry fashion the flight of stairs going up to the upper floor and the stairs that went down into the bowels of the building.

The phone continued to ring. He checked his watch. It was six o'clock in the evening. That could only mean one thing. Simon was calling. His Simon, with a glass of red in hand. He must hurry before the message bank kicked in.

He didn't think about last night's intruders. His thoughts were solely on Simon. His hand was on the doorknob, preparing to turn it, when the phone stopped ringing and a voice floated down the stairs.

"Hello, gorgeous."

It was a man's voice. If Orestes was honest with himself he would have said it was his own voice, speaking on his own mobile phone. Except the voice was stronger, more assured than his own had ever been. Spoken from deep inside the chest, instead of the throat. But his mind wouldn't go there. Even so, the terror that washed over him was paralyzing. The man was still upstairs, an imposter, pretending to be him, and he was speaking to Simon. Simon who didn't know better and would doubtless play along.

"Missing you, of course," the man said. "How are you?"

The man walked nimbly across the top of the stairs toward the kitchen with the phone to his ear.

"Hold on. Just going to get a glass of wine."

Laughter. The same easy release of jubilation from the throat. Orestes envisaged the man's face relax into it, showing the large even teeth. The spark of green eyes beneath heavy brows.

"I'll put you on speaker."

And suddenly Simon's voice came through, loud and clear.

"Oh, hurry, baby. I'm dying to have a swig of this alcohol. It's been a full-on day."

Together they laughed, the man and Simon, as though they had always known each other and it would be ever thus.

Determined to put a stop to the charade, Orestes tried to open the door. It was locked. It did not open. He put his shoulder to it, shouted, and pounded the wood on either side of the glass but it was no good. The door did not budge. No one heard and no one came. And all the while the man upstairs spoke to Simon on the phone as if he had a right to, and when Orestes stopped making a racket he heard Simon's deep, steady voice drift down the stairs to caress his ears as he recounted his day and questioned the man about this and that.

"It really is wonderful up here," Simon said. "Nice and sunny. Today was twenty-two degrees, would you believe. I wish you'd come."

"That's what I was going to tell you," the man replied. "I'm driving up first thing tomorrow morning."

Orestes didn't know what appalled him most. The pronouncement or Simon's ecstatic cries. He went on and on, whooping in the phone until the speakers crackled.

"I'm sick of the cold here," the man added. "It hasn't stopped raining since you left."

"The heavens are crying because we're apart." Simon chuckled.

That's when Orestes tried to put his fist through the glass in the door. Nothing happened. It was as hard and unyielding as granite. All that happened was a searing pain shot through his knuckles, wrist, and into the arm. He fell back, gritting his teeth, tears in his eyes.

He remained welded to the door for as long as the conversation lasted. Then the man hung up and went about the business of preparing a meal, behaving as if he belonged there. That he had every right.

Later still, he descended the stairs, walked right past the painting without so much as glancing at it, to collect a small suitcase from the studio-garage. He returned upstairs and Orestes heard him pack, from within the confines of his own prison, his immurement, before going early to bed, presumably so that he could make an early start.

The man left the house at six-thirty in the morning. He had a quick coffee while listening to the morning news on the radio and then he was out of the door.

Orestes watched from behind the glass panel as the man turned at the entrance to cast a final eye over the interior, before turning off the hall light. Then he opened the front door and stepped out. A fine rain fell around the streetlight across the street. The man closed the front door and Orestes heard him lock the security gate before the brown Ford sedan parked on the footpath started. Orestes knew the man would have to let the car warm up before setting off, and that's what he did, without having to be told. As if he knew and the car belong to him, not Orestes. Then the vehicle moved away from the pavement and all was quiet.

An eerie hush fell over the house. From his vantage point, Orestes saw the stairs going up and the stairs going down. In the gloom he saw a narrow wedge of the upstairs and a slightly larger portion of the downstairs. As minutes passed, the house he knew and loved seemed to grow colder, more distant and unfamiliar. It was as though it, too, forgot his presence and warmth between the walls and would in time encompass another, without so much as missing Orestes or thinking about him again.

Now, he thought, *the secret life of houses begins.*

Nothing out of the ordinary happened. Nothing skulked out of a dark corner to cross the floor on stealthy legs. No new sounds emerged, except that the familiar creaks and pops were magnified. No fresh revelations presented themselves. Only a gentle wind came out of the studio and swept the floor. A cobweb high up under the ceiling swayed like a pendulum in a breeze. The chimes struck a graceful note. Light shifted across walls and fell on floors, stronger here, weaker there, with the passage of time. Day became night. And night became day. People walked on the street, stopped outside to talk, moved on. Trains shunted past every fifteen minutes. Rain fell. He even heard Robin and Diane talk in the house next door.

He knew it was only a matter of time. All he had to do was wait.

Chapter Eleven

Late Saturday afternoon, the front door opened and the double entered with Simon behind him. Light filled the entrance hall. Life and warm bodies brought the house to life. It stirred and pressed around them, like a skin.

The double placed his bag on the floor. Then he turned and grabbed Simon in his arms and carried him over the threshold into the house.

Simon wrapped his arms around the man's neck and laughed, delighted. "Oh, so forceful."

"You like it?"

"You bet. Are you going to ask me to marry you?"

"Why not? We can now…"

"I thought you weren't the marrying kind."

"Things change."

The double set Simon down in the entrance.

"That's unlike you," Simon said, tilting his head to one side. "You've changed." He looked handsome in his black jeans with white stitching and a black leather jacket, zipped up to the throat against the cold.

Orestes's heart leaped at the pronouncement. Simon would recognize the fraud and come up the stairs to open the door and release him from prison.

"New me," the double replied, taking Simon in his arms. "I'm not letting you out of my sight again."

"I like the sound of that…"

The men kissed. Then Simon turned on the overhead light. Orestes saw that the double definitely, without doubt, resembled him in all respects. If he didn't know better, he would say the man was him. Unequivocally. Certainly, Simon seemed to think so.

Yet there was something different about him too. It was an undefinable quality. The eyes sparked with energy, more life. His voice boomed. It was more confident. Orestes swallowed his words. But there was greater force behind each word this man spoke. He stood upright, appeared taller, and he held back his shoulders, so that his chest was pushed out; and when he walked he took longer, more certain strides. He didn't cast down his eyes, afraid and hunched. The opposite of how Orestes carried himself.

"It's good to be home," Simon said, wrapping his arms around the double again and kissing him on the lips.

The double wrapped his arms around Simon's waist and returned a deeper kiss. To Orestes it was indecent, the way the men leaned into each other, the double claiming Simon's lips as his own, and Simon seemed to like it. To want it. The force of it. The pressure Orestes had never dared apply in case Simon break or be repulsed and turn away.

They stepped away from each other and the double said, "How about I bring up the bags and you make hot coffee?"

"You're on."

Simon began to ascend the stairs when he stopped.

"Oh," he said, staring at the painting. "You changed it."

The double came to stand beside him, looking up at the painting of the door. "I thought it needed something."

"You painted your face in the glass."

"Yes," the double said without hesitation.

"Why does it look so strange?"

"Because you're looking at the face through bubble wrap. Have a closer look."

Simon did.

The miracle of it! The wonder of his nearness. Simon brought his face up close to Orestes's own face until Orestes was sure he was going to nuzzle up to him and see the situation for what it was.

Surely now, Orestes thought, *he will denounce the other guy.*

Nothing of the sort happened. Simon only continued to stare at Orestes with inquiring eyes, leaning closer to study the technique the double had deployed to achieve the desired effect of seeing an object through bubble wrap. Orestes felt Simon's breath on his skin. He breathed in and imagined that he smelled his partner's tangy aftershave and felt the familiar heat of his flesh. At one point he even thought he had come up close for a kiss.

His heart almost broke when Simon stepped back and pulled a face.

"I see what you've done," he said. "It's clever. But it's also creepy." He turned to the double. "I hope you don't expect me to walk past that on the way to the toilet every night."

The man laughed. "I'll take it down if it scares you."

"It's a great painting. It's just that it's disturbing now. I'll get used to it."

Simon freed himself from the double's hold and continued to ascend the stairs in the light way he had of taking the steps. The double followed more heavily with the suitcases.

From inside the painting, Orestes thought the man who had replaced him in his own house looked content, happy to be stepping into his shoes as he labored under the weight of the cases. Perhaps two days in Mildura had done him good. Orestes was sure he had seen color in the cheeks.

For a time, he heard the two of them move back and forth over his head. Simon making coffee, putting on his favorite CD. The double placing the cases in the bedroom and emptying out his dirty clothes.

Orestes knew he ought to be horrified. He ought to panic and scream and demand to be let out. But something had shifted in him. He was paralyzed with indecision and with the inevitability of the situation. He couldn't do anything except let it play out. See where it went.

Later, the double came to stand at the top of the stairs, coffee cup in hand, to further assess the painting. Just by his proximity, the mere act of looking at Orestes, he seemed to drain his surrogate of vitality. There was no will to fight. And even as Orestes stood behind the door, thinking this, he felt himself fade. It was as though he was paper-thin, ephemeral as the breezes that inched across the floor when the house thought it was unoccupied and unwatched.

"You really think," the double said, taking a sip of coffee, "that the face is a mistake?"

Simon's voice was unequivocal. "Yes."

The double pursed his lips and nodded. "You're probably right," he said after a while. "It's a matter of knowing when to stop."

He set the coffee cup aside and descended the stairs. Simon came to stand at the top of the stairs behind him, having changed into a long, black dressing gown and blue slippers.

"You have to know when enough is enough," Simon said. "One brushstroke too many and you can kill a painting."

The man stared at Orestes's face in the glass as if studying a specimen in a jar. "I'll paint over it in the morning."

Orestes and the man stared at each other. They stared deep into each other's eyes. After a while Orestes didn't know which of them was the real Orestes Gallanos. And that scared him more than anything else so far.

Then another question coursed through his mind. *Does it matter?* The answer was immediate.

Of course it matters, he thought. *You will never hold Simon in your arms again. That matters more than anything else.*

He locked eyes with the man and hoped to somehow convey a message. This was not acceptable. It will not happen. And then he realized that he merely waited. He wasn't sure what he waited for. Perhaps an acknowledgment, one final sly wink before the deal was sealed between them. The switch made. Or perhaps he waited for the day when black pigments blotted him out.

That's when a hand fell on his shoulder from behind.

He spun around to see who it was, and the last thing he heard from the outside world was Simon's voice saying, "Did you hear that? Someone's crying."

THE BOY BY THE

GATE

It was a rainy night, and the four of us—Ross Orr, Geoff Hitchens, Rebecca Nagy, and me—had gathered round the fireplace at Rebecca's home to stay warm and keep each other company during the longest and coldest night of the year. As happens at this sort of gathering, what with one thing and another, people began to tell ghost stories. Real ghost stories. Things that happened to them or to a close friend.

As Ross related a particularly gruesome tale about a driver who encounters a gray woman on a lonely country road, Rebecca shuddered and, excusing herself, went to the kitchen to fetch more of her excellent chocolate cookies. As a tribute to her culinary skills, they were devoured in no time, and the plate had to be replenished, together with cups of hot Belgian cocoa.

Next in line was Geoff with an unsettling story from his childhood. Between the ages of ten and eleven, he awoke every night to find a blond boy standing at the foot of the bed. Nothing ever happened. The scene merely repeated itself, night after night, over many years, until Geoff was used to the visitant and did not bat an eyelid when the phantom made his appearance. In adulthood, Geoff discovered that a child of the same description died in that room more than thirty years earlier.

Being the close-minded sort, I had nothing in the way of phantasmal visitations to offer, which meant I could pass the ball with relief to our hostess. Rebecca remained quiet for a minute or two. Then she raised her dark head and said, "This didn't happen to me. It happened to a friend long ago, when she and I were in our last year of high school. If I hesitate it's because I'm not sure I have a right to tell the story to a group of strangers who didn't know her and can't possibly appreciate the seriousness of what happened to her at a young age..."

She trailed off, and her face clouded. Our murmured protests and encouragements were met with an inflexible silence. Rebecca's expression was eloquent. It said the story she was thinking of relating to this comic gathering was no light entertainment. It had obviously left a deep and lasting impression on her psyche.

"Come on, Beck, out with it," Ross, always the gregarious one, said. "It'll do you good to get it off your chest."

She smiled sadly. "I doubt that."

The fire crackled in the grate, and rain lashed the windows as we waited for her to reach a decision.

I studied Ross and Geoff as they sat in armchairs on the other side of the coffee table and saw that the high spirits had left them. Rebecca's disturbed mood pervaded the atmosphere and affected the entire company. It was as though the specter of a dreadful past hovered over us like a storm cloud.

After some minutes, Rebecca stood from her seat beside me, threw a log in the fire, and said, "If I'm going to do this, I'll do it properly. You see, I found out about it from a letter my friend Alice Kendall addressed to me before she...before...well, before it all happened. I don't think I could do the story justice if I told it in my own words. It's best if I read the letter to you, if that's all right...? She was a talented writer—wanted to become a novelist." She cast questioning eyes round the room, and the three of us gratified her with a nod. "Excuse me a minute while I get it."

She was gone for about ten minutes, during which time Ross, Geoff, and I contemplated our own thoughts.

The wind howled outside. The jacaranda tree hissed as it thrashed and tossed against the windowpane, the bare branches flung about like the arms of a demented skeleton. A part of me wished to be safely in the guest room upstairs, instead of playing silly buggers with adults who ought to know better. As I said, I am a cynic and very skeptical about supernatural occurrences. It was all I could do to stop myself from laughing or sneering at the circle of glum faces.

I was about to announce that I was going to bed when Rebecca returned with an envelope.

"Sorry, I had trouble finding it," she said, reclaiming her seat beside me. She opened the envelope and removed several sheets of thin, crackling, and somewhat yellowed paper. These were carefully unfolded and placed in her lap.

"Before I read Alice Kendall's words," Rebecca said, "I should tell you that all this happened at Port Fairy in the winter of 1986. It's a pretty little town on the west coast of Victoria. Alice had gone there with her father, Barnaby Kendall. He was an academic, speaking at a literary conference. He had taken his only daughter along for a relaxing week at the seaside. Alice's mother had passed away a year earlier." Rebecca raised her eyes and looked at each of us. Content with our undivided attention, she added, "And so to the letter. I'll leave out any parts that don't directly relate to the story."

She picked up the sheets and began to read in a voice that betrayed no emotion and yet provided the perfect accompaniment to the crackling of the logs in the fireplace and the shrieking of the wind outside. As she progressed with the tale, however, her voice gained a deeper, darker edge with rapid alterations in the registry of delivery. It mixed with the sound of rainwater gurgling in the drainpipes so that, by the time Rebecca finished reading, it seemed we listened to a lament for the dead or a funeral rite. To this day, I shudder to think of it.

Dear Becky,

On Friday night Dad was invited to dinner with people who are part of the literary festival. I had some stuff to do beforehand, so I promised to join him half an hour later. We are staying at a quaint place called the Merrijig Inn by the Moyne River. It's old and a bit run down but comfortable and it has heaps of atmosphere—you know, the kind of place where crusty fishermen crashed for the night before going out to sea the next morning. Dad estimated that it'd take me about ten minutes to walk from the inn to the house where the dinner was on Regent Street, across the other side of town.

It was dark by the time I left. Port Fairy is a pretty town, with wide tree-lined streets and cute stone cottages tucked away in well-tended gardens. The thought of walking through the empty streets on my own didn't faze me at all. The guy at the reception desk asked if I'd be all right. I told him I was fine. The sky was clear, and a bitter wind prickled my skin. The air smelled of fresh brine and woodsmoke, and there was a constant boom of surf coming from the back beach. It sounded like cannon fire. I stuck my hands in my pockets, hunkered down in my coat, and set off at a trot, virtually hopping from one distant streetlight to the next.

When I reached the center of town, where all the shops are, I decided it would be quicker to cut through the churchyard at St. John's rather than walk the long way round to Regent Street. I know, famous last words. But it was so lovely and peaceful, and I felt so good and safe walking under the bright stars that I really didn't think anything of it.

I was standing on the nature strip, about to cross the narrow street and enter the churchyard, when I noticed something by the bluestone gate.

At first, I thought it was a white balloon, hovering above the ground at about the height of a small child. Then I realized that what I took to be the light shining off white latex was, in fact, a face.

A boy's face.

I was startled at first and then intrigued.

He was incredibly pale and rigid as a statue. I was thinking a kid that young shouldn't be out on his own at this time of night, when I noticed his clothes. He wore an ill-fitting, old-fashioned jacket; heavy three-quarter length pants tucked in thick socks; and scuffed boots that were too big for him. His hair was dirty blond and messy.

Even as I stared at him, I could tell he was no ordinary boy. He was too still and vivid for that, as though he was some kind of high-fidelity projection put on freeze-frame. He even juddered a little at the edges, as though someone had paused a video. I was about to say hello to him when he turned and not so much as walked but glided very rapidly behind the gatepost into the churchyard.

"Hey, don't go in there," I called. "It's dark." I ran after him, but he was nowhere in sight. He completely vanished. A quick search yielded nothing.

I didn't tell Dad. Next morning, straight after breakfast at eight-thirty, I ran across town to the church, and there was the boy, waiting. In cold streaming sunlight that fell in dapples through the tree canopy, dressed in the same clothes, and standing at exactly the same spot, as if he'd been there all night.

The street was deserted; the houses closed up. I stood on the wet nature strip and studied his bloodless face. There was no indication that he saw me. The pale-blue eyes seemed impossibly remote, as if he saw beyond this world into an altogether different plane. After a minute, in repetition of the previous night, he pivoted on the spot and disappeared behind the gatepost. Only this time, in daylight, I noticed something peculiar about the way he moved. It was as if he were a figure on a cuckoo clock, being shunted out on the axis of a mechanical arm and then whipped back again. It was alarming and frightening, too, because it robbed him of any humanity.

I searched the grounds for a long time. There was nothing to find and, on the wide-open lawn, no place for him to hide. The church was locked so I couldn't make inquiries. A man stood smoking under a verandah across the street, but he didn't look like he'd welcome queries about peculiar children.

The important thing is, Becky, I wasn't afraid. Just puzzled. The poor thing looked so sad and lonely, and I wanted to help. I was convinced he was trapped on that spot for some reason, repeating the same action over and over again. For all eternity. Who knew how long he'd been there?

It was up to me to break the spell and free him.

At ten o' clock I went to a nearby bookshop and spoke to a woman with a black ponytail and beautiful silvery eyes. Her name was Jo. She was understandably perplexed by the story and said that, as far as she knew, no one had seen anything of that description in the churchyard. All the same, she picked a history of Port Fairy from a nearby bookshelf and leafed through it.

"Here," she said after consulting several dusty books, "listen to this..."

It turns out George O'Dowd, a fisherman, saw the boy by the gate in 1876. Marilyn McNally made the next sighting in 1916. The final recorded sighting was in 1946. The witness was Tony Wright, a war veteran who lived behind the church in Barclay Street. In all cases, Jo read from the book, the witnesses reported that the boy ducked into the churchyard and vanished.

I asked Jo if there were any theories about who the boy might be. She read from the book.

"Many believed the ghostly boy was Davey Adair, a nine-year-old orphan who did odd jobs around town in the early 1860s. It was a severe winter. One night the boy sought shelter inside St. John's church. A heartless caretaker turned him out. Next morning, Davey was found frozen solid beside the Barclay Street gate. In death he received what had been denied him in life. His young body was buried in consecrated ground just inside the gate."

"Here, look," Jo said and pointed at an ink drawing on one page.

At one stage the faithful were buried in St. John's churchyard. What is now a nice green lawn was once filled with tombstones, leaning every which way.

"What happened to the graves?" I asked Jo.

She shrugged. "The bodies were interred and moved to the Port Fairy Cemetery on the other side of the highway."

"Davey too?"

"Probably."

Despite the terrible story, I was thrilled to have found this much information about the boy. Now that I knew his name, I could help him.

"And I'm only the fourth person to see him," I said, trying not to sound too thrilled.

"I wouldn't jump to conclusions," Jo mumbled, her eyes still on the book. "They're only the sightings that were reported. There could be others that weren't."

Good point. "Well, thanks," I said, turning to leave.

"Not so fast," she said, grabbing my arm. "The book says that strange things happened to the people who saw the boy. I'd be careful if I were you."

"What strange things?"

She shrugged again. "Don't know. It just says, 'Strange and peculiar occurrences befell the unfortunates who witnessed the apparition.' Please be careful."

"You believe me, then?" I said to her with a smile.

*"Don't see why you'd make up a story like this."
She was a very practical woman, and I liked her
a lot.*

*That evening Dad had to attend yet another one
of those endless dinners people are obliged to go
to when appearing at literary events. This one
was at the pub on Sackville Street, round the
corner from St. John's church.*

*It was a bleak night, with the promise of rain.
Wind boomed overhead and it was freezing cold.
Dad and I were about to step into the warmth of
the pub when I said, "Dad, can you give me a
minute? I want to check on something," and
before he answered I ran the few meters to
Barclay Street and up to the church gates.*

*Davey Adair was waiting for me in his usual spot,
as unnervingly still as ever. In the wan electric
light that filtered through the thick canopy of
trees, he seemed to be made of crackling frost.*

*I kneeled on the grass and stretched out my
hands.*

*"Davey Adair," I said in my best voice. "My name
is Alice. I'm your friend. Please let me help you, if
I can."*

*There was no response or even a flicker of
awareness. Except that the juddering round his*

figure intensified. Then, again, he pivoted on the spot like a mechanical toy on a spring and merged with the greater darkness behind the gate.

Disappointed, I ran back to Dad. I was at the corner of Barclay Street when I stopped and, for some reason, looked back at the church. Davey Adair's shiny moon-like face poked out and studied me from behind the bluestone wall.

"Good," I thought. "I got through to you."

When I reached my ever-patient father at the pub door, Davey stood at the corner of Barclay and Bank Streets, staring at me. Even though I knew he didn't mean any harm, it was a bit unnerving. His pupils looked as if they'd been painted on his eyelids.

"Who's the boy?" Dad asked.

"Oh, no one," I said, pushing him inside.

He gave me a knowing look and left it at that.

That was four hours ago, dear Becky, my bestest friend in the world. I'm now in my room at the Merrijig Inn, writing this letter to you. Dad is asleep next door. The rain is pelting down, and the gale coming off the ocean is enough to put the wind up Captain Ahab.

Becky, something has been scratching at the window for a half hour. I daren't look. The room is upstairs on the first floor. It can only be a branch from the big tree outside. Even so, I'm spooked.

Davey was on the street when Dad and I returned to the inn tonight. I caught sight of him as we came in the front door, and then I saw him again from my window. He stood under the streetlight on the opposite pavement, looking up at me. That little head tilted up. The pale throat exposed. The mouth moving as if forming words. But of course, from this distance, I couldn't hear a thing. I must admit the idea that he followed me is freaking me out a bit. And then getting a glimpse of his mouth contorting in that awful way, as if he's forgotten how to perform perfectly normal bodily functions, gave me the serious heebie-jeebies.

I'm sitting at the small desk, wondering what I got myself into.

Becky, when the mouth opened, it was just a black hole that went all the way to the center of his being. Poor thing. It started to rain, and the water fell in his open mouth as if it were a well or a bucket or something. He didn't seem to notice.

There's that horrible scritch-scratch of busy little hands at the window again.

Scritch-scratch; scritch-scratch.

It sounds like broken nails being dragged against glass. And it's driving me insane.

When I look up from the letter, I see over the well-made bed to the window with the pretty lace curtains gathered at the side. It's not a large room. It's quite small, actually, built into the attic, with a dormer window, which is why I can clearly see Davey Adair floating, yes, floating one floor up, outside the rain-streaked glass. The hair is plastered to his forehead, and one hand reaches out to press the window. He reminds me of an abandoned puppy, begging to be let in.

All the same, it's a terrifying sight. And yet, for some reason, I feel terribly sorry for him. My heart goes out to him. It almost breaks at the pitiful sight of him out there, alone and abandoned. He looks how I felt after Mom died. Shattered and lost and bewildered and in need of a friend.

Maybe that's what he wants, Becky. A friend.

If only his eyes weren't so lifeless. I'd fling open the window and say, "Come in, Davey, come in. I'll take care of you. You can stay with me forever."

His mouth moved again. I think he's trying to tell me something. If only it wasn't so black, like the coal chute at my grandmother's place.

All right. I've made up my mind. I've been sitting here for the longest time, trying to decide what to do. Now I know.

Hold on, Becky. I'm going to lay down the pen and open the window. I can't stand that scratching any more. And I must hear what he has to say. Hopefully he'll stop making that keening noise once he's out of the cold and in this warm, bright room.

I'm putting down the pen now, Becky. Wait for me, won't you? I'll be back in a tick…

Rebecca set the letter on the coffee table and looked up. There were tears in her eyes.

"She never came back," she said in a choked voice.

Ross leaned forward and said, "That's it?"

"Yes. She didn't finish the letter."

"But what happened to Alice?" Ross pursued.

Rebecca stared at the wall behind him and shrugged. "She disappeared. Hasn't been seen since. Next morning her father alerted the police. There was an investigation. Nothing was found, and, of course, everyone dismissed the letter as pure fantasy.

"The only sighting—if you can call it that—came late the next morning. A parishioner on the way to church found a pair of shoes embedded in the ground just inside St. John's gates. Turned out they belonged to Alice. Poor Barnaby Kendall returned to Melbourne with his daughter's suitcase and a pair of crushed, muddied shoes. He died of sorrow not long after, believing he'd taken his daughter to her death."

"What do you mean 'embedded'?" Ross asked. For a sensitive man, he could be callous at times.

Rebecca sipped her cocoa before answering. "Just that. The shoes were half buried in the soil, toes first, like someone was trying to bury them."

Ross whistled between his teeth and said, "Or like something dragged her under the ground, and the shoes came off with the force of the impact."

Rebecca grimaced. "Don't. That's too horrible."

"There was no evidence in her room at the inn?" Ross pursued his line of inquiry.

Rebecca shook her head. "The window to Alice's room was open. The rain got in and made a mess of the place. This letter was almost soaked through. The police said she'd probably run away with the boy her father had seen, but I don't know... She wasn't the sort. Studied hard, got top grades in just about everything. You know the type."

"You don't seriously think a ghost called Davey Adair took her," I put in.

"Well, what do you think happened then?" Ross called out. His eyes lit up as if he was about to punch me for daring to challenge what everyone appeared to accept without question.

"I don't know what happened, Ross," I replied. "I just don't believe she's being held captive by a bugaboo. And now," I said, gathering my cup and saucer, "if you don't mind, I'm off to bed. It's late."

Geoff, who had been quiet since Rebecca finished reading the letter, looked up from contemplating the embers in the fireplace. "I reckon we should all go to Port Fairy and see if the ghost is still there," he said.

"Well, if you do," I put in, "you go without me."

"I always wanted to," Rebecca said in a distant voice. "I was just too scared to go on my own."

Geoff saw his chance and grabbed it. "What self-respecting goth would turn down the opportunity to see a ghost? Are we going or what, team?"

"Count me in," Ross said. "I'll drive us up there tomorrow. It'll take about three hours in this crap weather."

"You don't drive," Geoff reminded him.

"Oh, yeah," Ross said. "You can drive then."

"I don't have a car," Geoff added.

"I'll drive," Rebecca offered in a frustrated voice.

And because we are and have always been a band of four, I was compelled to say that I, too, would go with them to a distant seaside town whose wide avenues and well-preserved cottages have seen more of life's beauty and savagery than most places in Australia.

Maybe the boy by the gate claimed his last victim in Alice Kendall. Maybe he still waits.

"If nothing else," I said to Rebecca, "you might find out what happened to your friend."

At that moment, the window casement flew open with a crash, and all the wild restlessness and ruin of the night rushed into the civilized room. A gust of wind picked up the letter on the coffee table and hurled it in the fireplace. Everyone leaped to their feet with cries of shock and alarm.

"No, no." Rebecca jumped at the fire to save her friend's memento.

It was useless. The letter was reduced to ash in a matter of seconds. Feathery blackened pieces of paper floated up the chimney and disappeared. Geoff put an arm round her shoulders and pulled her away from the gutting flames.

It fell to me to close the window and return order to the room. I fought past the crazily flapping curtains and extended both arms into the feral night to close the wooden shutters. As I did so, ice-cold fingers locked round my wrists like shackles and long nails scraped my skin. Startled, I let out a yelp and leaped back. In doing so, I caught a glimpse of the storm-tossed garden and the thing Rebecca's letter had summoned to this house.

"What is it?" Ross cried. He pushed me aside and quickly closed the window.

Calm returned to the room as though a switch had been thrown. The curtains settled in their usual place against the wall. Rain glistened on furniture. A palm frond trembled in a corner. Rebecca wept against Geoff 's shoulder, and Ross stood over me, asking why I had screamed.

But I couldn't tell him. For the life of me I couldn't...

Nor could I stop hearing that awful *scritch-scratching* at the window.

IN THE DARK

Chapter One

WERRIBEE POLICE STATION
5:15 P.M. AUGUST 16, 1991

Police will not comment on whether a secret cult is responsible for scenes of carnage uncovered in Jackson's Cove, west of Melbourne. Dozens of bodies were discovered in the remote fishing community. Two unidentified people were found alive at the scene. It is not yet clear if they are victims or the perpetrators. One is in a critical condition in hospital and the other in police custody. Investigations are ongoing.

Doctor Khaled Sidawi sighed and handed the newspaper to Superintendent Amanda Cribbe. She folded it and set it aside.

They stood in front of a two-way mirror, staring into a bright room that contained a table and two chairs. Their eyes were fixed on a seated figure wrapped in a gray blanket. Only the boy's head showed. It resembled boiled beetroot.

"I suppose he's one of the two people you found at the cove," Sidawi remarked.

Cribbe, a tall redhead in a black pants suit, folded her arms and nodded.

"Why is his face red?"

"Blood."

"You haven't cleaned him yet?"

"He goes nuts if anyone goes near him."

"What about his parents?"

Cribbe cleared her throat and said, "Adopted. They don't want to know."

"Good Samaritans are the worst."

"That's quite an observation for a child psychologist, doc."

"Born of experience. What do you want from me, Amanda?"

The friendship between the two went back to university days. Sidawi, usually a reticent man, could afford to be direct with Cribbe. She was herself a straight-down-the-line woman.

"He's been like this since we found him, Khaled." Cribbe nodded at the boy. "Hasn't said a word."

"When?"

"About nine hours ago."

"Looks like he's traumatized." Sidawi scrutinized the kid through the protective one-way glass. "What's his name?"

Cribbe consulted a file and struggled to pronounce the boy's name.

"What a mouthful," she added. "I yearn for the days when crims had easy to pronounce names like Bill."

Sidawi frowned, took the paper from her, and looked it over. "Orestes Gallanos," he said. "It's not that hard, you know."

"Easy for you to say."

"Your girlfriend's name is Giulietta and you can't pronounce Orestes?"

Cribbe smiled. "I just call her Julie."

Sidawi shook his head. "According to Aeschylus," he said, handing back the notepad, "Orestes killed his mother Clytemnestra and her lover, and was set upon by the Furies."

"Looks like it too." Cribbe nodded grimly at the sight behind the glass. "Anyway, he's thirteen years old."

"Looks a lot younger than that."

"Small for his age. Been living on the streets for about two years. Malnourishment is the least of his problems. He has a record. Burglary, drugs, soliciting for the purposes of prostitution. You name it.

"What we want to know," Cribbe went on, "is what has he got to do with this business at Jackson's Cove. A statement of some sort may help us get to the bottom of it. But he won't talk. I thought you could help, being a wog and all."

They grinned in good humor at each other.

"Because," he said, "a Lebanese Muslim is..."

"The same as a Greek," she finished off for him.

They grinned at each other again. He shook his head again and rolled his eyes.

"Right," he said. "Let's get started."

"Hold on. Ask him if he knows this person." Cribbe pointed to two words written on a sheet of paper. "Might help."

Sidawi memorized the name written in the notepad and nodded. Cribbe opened the door to the interrogation room and ushered him in.

"I want to be alone with him."

Cribbe nodded, closed the door behind Sidawi, and went to turn on the speaker that allowed her to listen in on the conversation.

Sidawi advanced into the room, sat on a green plastic chair opposite the boy and, after studying him for a moment, introduced himself.

"Orestes," he said, keeping his voice low, "I want to help. Don't be afraid. You're safe."

Pale eyes fixed on Sidawi's face. Dilated pupils. Stiff, matted hair crowned the gaunt head. It looked as if someone had taken the kid by the heels and dipped him in a vat of gore.

"Can you tell me what happened?"

When the boy did not respond, Sidawi said, "Orestes, does the name Sid Jarvis mean anything to you?"

"Sid?" Orestes mumbled. His head pivoted from side to side, as if he expected to see the owner of the name standing in a corner.

"That's right. Sid Jarvis. Do you know him?"

Orestes opened his mouth and began to talk in a halting manner. He mumbled, tripped over words, swallowed others, got confused, stopped, and started again. But he spoke with such intensity that he pulled Sidawi into an increasingly bizarre narrative that for all intents and purposes still played out in the boy's mind.

"It started when we went to Jackson's Cove."

"Why did you go there?"

"For a job."

"What sort of a job?"

The boy stopped and fumbled around in the confused confines of his mind.

Sidawi said, "Go on, Orestes."

After a while, the boy continued...

Chapter Two

JACKSON'S COVE
10:39 P.M. AUGUST 15, 1991

"I'm not saying it's a done deal," Sid said. "I'm just saying let's see what happens. Okay?"

"We don't know anything about this guy," Orestes replied.

"Won't be the first time."

"True," Orestes mumbled, but he doubted Sid heard him above the roar of the sea and the hiss of coastal scrub tossed by the wind.

It was a cold night. They stood beside the blue sedan, taking the full blast coming off the bay. The sea was an invisible but palpable presence in the dark, highlighted here and there with occasional phosphorescent caps.

"Let's go," Orestes said. "It's freezing out here."

All the same it was a relief to be outside, to breathe fresh air. The interior of the stolen car had been hot and stuffy during the long drive. Orestes had felt queasy and nauseous. His head spun and he felt as if he was variously light and airless or being crushed under concrete. More than once he came close to throwing up. Rather than tell Sid to pull over so he could vomit on the roadside, he'd taken another swig of Coke from the plastic liter bottle, burped, and hoped for the best.

Sid flicked his cigarette away and followed the flying sparks across the empty carpark toward the cabins that lined the western side of the cove.

The chill cut through Orestes's denim jacket, primping his skin to gooseflesh. He crossed his arms over his chest and ran after Sid.

"Wait up." He burped again, tripped, kept going.

He was doing this job because they had no money and nowhere to sleep. Sid had found the man on a gay pickup bulletin board and struck a deal about which Sid was unusually cagey.

Orestes caught up with Sid and said, "What's that smell?"

"Fertilizer from the vegetable gardens up there."

"Up there" was the embankment behind the cabins. It was high and steep, with a rutted road that had brought them to a muddy patch of ground that passed for a carpark where the cabins ended. Vegetable gardens covered the flat land for miles beyond.

"Stinks like shit."

Sid flashed the torch he carried at a piece of paper in his hand. "Look for bungalow eighteen and quit yapping."

"It's probably that one." Orestes pointed at a simple wooden structure about a quarter of the way along. A lonesome lightbulb shone on a blue door. All the other cabins were in darkness.

The sandy path in front of the cabins was so narrow they had to walk in single file—vegetation on the left, cabins on the right. All of them appeared to be locked and deserted for winter, a line of gray sentinels on the watch.

Orestes said, "A hangout for desperadoes."

"We should move in."

They chuckled and hurried along, huddled against the cold.

The entire length of the windswept coast—almost a mile—was filled with fibro huts that sat on the sand, sea spray and foliage at the doorstep. A strip of unkempt tarmac ran on at an elevated level behind the cabins, separating them from the vegetable plots covering the land beyond—land flat and lonesome as the Nullabor, the well-lit suburbs having stopped miles earlier. On the road to Jackson's Cove, Orestes had seen only three brick houses plonked in the middle of more vegetable gardens, beat-up utes and chained dogs prowling under porch lights. It was another world.

"Do people live here?"

"In summer," Sid said. "Not now."

Orestes put a hand on Sid's shoulder.

"I feel kinda sick..." He wavered on his feet and clapped his hand across his mouth to stop the vomit.

Sid faced Orestes.

"Look, if you don't want to come, go back to the car and wait." He took the keys out of his pocket and jangled them in front of Orestes's face. "But stop whining. You're getting on my nerves. *I'm sick*," he mimicked.

Orestes pushed away the keys. "I don't want to wait in the car. I just don't feel good, that's all." When he saw this was not getting him anywhere, he added, "Tell me what this guy wants."

"He said he likes to watch."

Orestes rolled his eyes. Great. Another weirdo.

"It'll be an easy two hundred bucks."

"Heard that before," Orestes said.

All the same he trusted Sid. He was a good ten years older than Orestes. They had known each other for almost a year and Sid had not let Orestes down once.

"Don't worry, princess," Sid said. "I'll look after you."

He pulled a knife out of his black leather jacket. It was a savage looking thing with a wooden handle and nasty serrated teeth.

Orestes hadn't seen it before. Putting on a mock shiver, he said, "Oh, I feel so safe."

"Have another sip." Sid proffered the Coke bottle Orestes had been guzzling from for the last hour. "It'll make you feel better."

Orestes gulped the now-warm, syrupy liquid and burped.

"Finish it off."

Careful eyes watched Orestes as he chugged the rest and threw away the bottle, stumbling as he went. He could barely stand and his stomach lurched as if he was on board a ship. Sounds were heightened, exaggerated, in his ears. Lights danced before his eyes. And the sea sounded like a jet plane taking off. If he didn't know better, he'd say he was high. But he hadn't taken anything.

They came to the cabin with the light bulb and the blue door. Sid knocked. Waited. No answer. Knocked again. Still no answer. The overhead light with the ceramic hood flickered each time he thumped the wood with a fist.

"Come on, open up," he said, shivering.

Orestes saw two moths flutter around the light before it sputtered and failed, plunging them in almost total darkness.

Sid stepped closer to the entry and said, "Hey, dude, it's me, Sid."

The door remained obstinately closed.

Orestes checked his watch. Ten-forty-five. What was he doing out here? Why wasn't he tucked up in a warm bed like a normal kid? Not that he could remember what "normal" was like. Two years on the street and already this was all he knew.

"We've been had," he said. "Again."

It was common in their line of work. Some poor schmuck makes a booking and then chickens out or someone with a bit more guts gets them to an isolated spot for a joke or to bash them up.

"Nah," said Sid. "This guy was genuine."

Orestes almost believed him. But then...

Panic came on stealthy legs. It grabbed him by the scruff of the neck and gave him a good shake, top to bottom, when he least expected it. He was so rattled, he grabbed Sid by the arm and pulled him away from the door.

"Get away from there," he said. "There *is* someone inside."

"That's what we want, numbskull. Someone in there. To let us in."

"I've got a bad feeling about this, Sid. I can *feel* him. Right here." He punched his stomach, almost bringing up the liquid he had swallowed. "And it feels bad. I'm serious. Let's get out of here."

"Dude, you're smashed." Sid caught himself. "I mean...you're stressed."

"I can hear something."

Sid stared at Orestes with hooded eyes, and for a second Orestes saw him in a way he had never seen him before—a sinister cast to the face. A suggestion of malevolence that was new. It made him wonder why he trusted Sid. Why he put so much faith in him when... The feeling evaporated, and he was left to wonder what prompted it.

Orestes let go of Sid and put his right ear to the door. At first there was only the sea and the sound of his own breath, his own pounding heart. Palms flat against peeling paint. Then a dawning awareness of something else. A presence? No, it was more like a pressure—a titanic force that pressed against the wood, causing it to swell under his hands. He pictured a hurricane or a typhoon trapped inside the shack and busting to get out.

"There's definitely someone in there."

A low undefinable sound, as if someone breathed moistly on the other side, caused Orestes to leap back.

"I heard something."

The isolation hit him hard. He looked around. They were far from anywhere. From lights, people. It was alien territory and he didn't like it. Not one bit. He looked around again and wished he was anywhere but here. For the first time in ages he wanted an adult to take charge. Do the right thing: take care of him. Not use him but look after him. Why couldn't Sid do that? Why couldn't he just say, "Let's get out of here."

"I don't feel safe," Orestes said, shaking his head. "It's a set up."

Like most street kids, Orestes had been bashed and robbed before.

"I'd like to see 'em try." Sid brandished the knife again. Without warning, he yelled, "Thanks for wasting my fucking time."

He kicked the door. Hinges rattled, the light came on, flickered once. Without warning, the bulb popped with an electric buzz. Glass rained on them.

"That's our cue," Orestes said, scampering away.

They started back to the car, Sid following Orestes. They managed to walk past two or three cabins when

Orestes heard the car engine. Headlights flashed on the high road behind the cabins, bounced on rusted, salt-encrusted tin roofs and the underside of dark pines thrashing in the gale; a vehicle navigated the gradient from road to carpark and pulled up beside the blue sedan.

"Cops," Sid yelped. He ducked behind a bush, pulling Orestes down with him.

It was a police car, high beams slicing the night open like a tin can. The passenger door opened and a uniform stepped out.

"Run," Orestes whispered.

Sid did not move. They crouched in the bushes outside a cabin with a green door. The entrance was ajar, revealing a pitch swath inside. Orestes was sure it had been closed earlier.

"That cabin's open," Sid murmured in his ear. "Hide in there until the pigs piss off."

Orestes nodded. There was maybe five or six feet of open space between their hiding place in the bushes and the cabin. If they were quick, they'd make it without being spotted, especially as it was dark out there, away from the parking lot.

A uniformed policeman flashed a torch in the interior of their car, tried the locked door. He was bulky with lamb-chop sideburns that joined to a huge handlebar mustache. His partner was younger, slimmer.

"I go first," Sid whispered. "Keep low to the ground so they don't see us."

Orestes nodded again.

Sid scrambled across on all fours. When he was inside, he beckoned from the doorway and Orestes followed. He was inside the cabin before he realized what he'd seen above the lintel.

The interior was end-of-the-world black. Zero visibility. He heard Sid breathe, carefully close the door, and lower a crossbar to secure the entrance. Both stood with their backs to the door, breathing hard.

"No lights," Sid whispered. "In case they come down here."

Several minutes passed. It did not look as if the cops were going to search the place.

The darkness in the cabin disturbed Orestes more than the cops outside. He was used to them. They were a known quantity. An occupational hazard. Solid darkness, on the other hand, was new to him. Unknown. His world was one of light, neon or electric, and when it was dark it was usually a theatrical darkness of necessity that owed as much to illumination as to darkness. One in which to conduct business.

He was so disturbed by the lack of light, so destabilized, he almost reached out to grab Sid's hand, to reassure himself that he was not alone in the void. To make things worse, he was feeling sick again and he needed to piss. His bladder was bursting and his head spun as if he sat on a merry-go-round in a playground—a long-ago playground, he remembered, in a green suburban corridor alongside his uncle and aunt's house as little Orestes played a solitary game, long after his mom and dad stepped out of his life.

"Listen," Sid hissed.

The car engine again.

"They're pissing off." Sid did a shuffling little dance in the dark. "Give it a minute and we'll fly, my man."

They heard the cop car pass on the road behind the cabin and go away. Sound faded. Then it was a matter of waiting until it was safe enough to get out of there.

Orestes was having trouble thinking straight. His thoughts were all over the place. Even so he said, "You know how we were meant to go to cabin eighteen?"

"Yeah."

"We went to the wrong one."

"How do you know?"

"We thought the cabin with the light was number eighteen. We went straight there, without checking numbers."

"How do you know it was the wrong one?"

"We're in cabin eighteen now. I saw the number above the door."

"Fuck me dead."

"Later, maybe..."

"You wish."

Their laughter was cut short by a new sound from outside. Shuffling footsteps approached and mounted the decking outside the door. Sandy boots scraped on wood. Someone tried the door. It shook on its hinges, rattled, but didn't open.

Orestes and Sid leaped away, silent as cats.

Orestes realized his mistake almost immediately. The wood at his back had been solid matter. It anchored him to the real world. Losing contact with it was like falling into space. Into nothing. He almost panicked and struggled for air.

"Quiet," Sid hissed from nearby.

Whoever was outside made one more feeble attempt at the door. It shook and stopped.

Orestes turned around and faced where he thought the entrance might be. The air was heavy, putrid. It was difficult to breathe and he was having trouble keeping his feet. His limbs grew heavy. Yet, at the same time, he was light, buoyant. As if he could levitate. Fly away... An anchor and a balloon at the same time. He felt great, as if the whole world was his friend and he loved everyone and everything in it. And yet, at the same time, it was out to kill him.

If he didn't know better he'd say he was totaled. But he hadn't taken anything. Had he?

"Did the cops come back?" he whispered, slurring.

He couldn't help himself; he was so scared he reached out toward where he thought Sid might be standing and grabbed his hand. It was glacial between his fingers. But it was better than nothing.

"The cops left," Sid whispered. "You heard 'em." His voice came from slightly to the left and in front of Orestes. "It's someone else."

"The owner of the cabin?"

"Oh, yeah." Sid's laugh was nervous. "I'll let him in."

Orestes heard Sid's footsteps move away from him, presumably toward the entrance, yet the hand remained firmly in his grasp. It didn't move at all.

He withdrew his own hand from the hand he'd been holding and said, "Sid, I think something's wr—"

He stopped talking when a muffled exchange came from the other side of the door.

"Shit, there's two of them," Sid whispered.

More scuffling was heard as two sets of feet left the deck and were heard to walk down the left side of the cabin, making their way to the rear of the building.

A male voice said, "Don't worry. He'll take care of 'em."

Another male voice responded with, "I wouldn't wanna swap places with them, that's for sure."

A laugh was followed by the murmur of the sea and the sound of coastal vegetation.

Sid's barely audible voice came out of the dark. "Hope there's no back door."

But Orestes wasn't paying attention. He was more bothered by the hand he'd been holding.

"Sid," he said, "turn your torch on for a sec."

He'd left everything he'd been carrying in the car in case the client bashed them and stole their stuff.

Orestes heard Sid approach. Seconds later, light leaped from the torch in Sid's palm, illuminating the underside of his face and throwing jagged shadows on the ceiling. Orestes was blinking against the glare when a voice said, "No lights."

An impression of a black gloved hand with a zipper at the wrist emerging from the gloom and knocking the torch to the ground. Startled, Sid yelped, jumped, tripped, and fell over backward. The back of his head hit something and he slumped to the floor. Orestes saw everything in a flash, moments before a heavy boot crushed the torch that lit the scene.

Blackness crashed in place like a bomb. But there had been time enough for Orestes to store information in a lucid part of his brain. What he saw stunned him.

The man's head was upside down. Hair that should have been on top of the head covered the lower portion of face and neck, while a clean-shaven dome pointed skywards.

How could that be?

He was paralyzed, still thinking about it when his bladder let go and warm liquid flooded his jeans.

Heart thumping, Orestes closed his eyes and recalled the scene in his mind's eye, trying to make sense of it.

He saw the man stand to the right of him. Legs. Torso. Shoulders. Head.

Orestes breathed a sigh of relief.

The man was dressed in black jeans. A black T-shirt covered a muscular upper body. The head was not upside down. It appeared that way in the failing light because a bushy red beard complimented a bald cranium. The face was covered by thick round goggles and, alarmingly, the man's scalp almost scraped a ceiling decorated with rows of gleaming hooks.

Orestes fought the urge to scream. Weirdly, curiosity and a sense of detachment replaced fear. He felt as though he was outside his body and yet, curiously, inside.

He wanted to know whose hand he'd been holding earlier. Had it been the tall man's? He was sure the other hand had not been sheathed in a glove.

Orestes closed his eyes again and tried to remember what he saw moments before the man killed Sid's torch. He pictured the length of his own left arm, the thin wrist, and then the hand with the long fingers. In those few seconds, he got as far as his own tapering fingertips and was beginning to form an impression of a blue, pulpy hand attached to a body hanging upside down from the ceiling when the voice said, "Strip."

It was a deep voice. Expensive brandy might sound like that if it talked.

Sid chose this moment to wake up. He groaned on the floor and said, "What happened?"

"I said 'Strip'."

"Tell me that was you," Sid said.

"I'm not saying it again. *Strip.*"

Orestes heard Sid stand up in the pitch black.

"Who are you?" Sid said in a weak voice. "What's going on?"

Orestes heard the man strike Sid hard across the face. The unexpected blow caused Sid to cry out and stumble. Orestes imagined him lifting a hand to his cheek before he said, "What the fuck?"

"Naked. Now."

More than anything, it was the calmness of the voice that freaked Orestes.

There was an element of calculation in Sid's voice when he said, "Mind turning on a light? Can't see a thing." He was obviously thinking of using the knife on the man.

"I like it in the dark."

"How you gonna see, man?"

A grim chuckle. "I see you."

Orestes stripped off his denim jacket and T-shirt and let them fall to the floor. Jeans followed. He rarely wore underwear on the job. For some reason, punters thought that was sexy. Unless of course they had a kink for underwear. Orestes had done all this before, countless times, usually for pudgy middle-aged guys who wanted to look at him and jerk off. Rarely did they want to touch. It was as if they were afraid of his youthful body or maybe they were awed by youth itself and didn't dare approach. With his hands covering his genitals, he felt more exposed than if the room was bathed in light and a dozen eyes were trained on him.

When Sid did not undress, the man said, "Listen, cunt, a nail gun is pointed at your noggin. If you're not buck naked in ten seconds, you're dead meat."

The hurried rustle of clothing indicated Sid's compliance.

The man said, "You're older than I expected, but this one—" Orestes shivered as a gloved hand caressed his right shoulder blade "—is perfect."

Orestes wished he could see. There must be a way out. He felt invisible in the dark. Yet he knew the man observed his every move; he must be wearing infra-red glasses. Orestes was disoriented and more scared than he had ever been. Even if he broke away, he was not sure in which direction to run. He thought the door was behind him or maybe to the right, but he wasn't sure. Was not sure of anything.

Besides, he couldn't leave Sid behind. They stuck together, no matter what.

The man said, "Don't move. I'm going to tie you up."

Orestes went rigid as a rough noose was dropped around his neck and tightened, the knot pressing against his Adam's apple. Then he felt the tension in the rope as it was similarly applied to Sid, linking them.

"That'll keep you together," the man said. Next, he addressed Sid. "Did you bring the knife?"

Slight hesitation. "Yes."

"The architect of his own destruction. Give it here."

Sid must have done as instructed because, shortly, Orestes felt the wooden handle of the blade slip between his own fingers.

"Rules," the man continued. "You fight to the death. I watch. There's a special prize for the winner." Pause. "Well," he added, "aren't you going to ask what the winner gets?"

The boys said nothing.

"Come on," the man teased. "Ask. Please, please, ask."

He was a child playing a game.

Orestes's voice cracked when he said, "What's the prize?"

The man sighed. "The winner gets to fuck the corpse before I put a couple of nails through his head. I film it all and sell it. There's a market for that kind of shit. There's a market for everything, if you know where to look."

The laughter was unbearable. It went on and on, growing in intensity until it filled the cabin. Orestes thought he might go mad and be saved from the horror. He began to whimper. He even thought maybe he should have stayed in that nice, clean suburban house with his uncle and aunt. Earlier, he had lost control of his bladder. Now he was afraid he was going to void his bowels.

Sid had not said a thing the whole time. It was as if he had gone away or maybe he had ceased to exist, leaving Orestes alone.

"You—" the gloved hand brushed the back of Orestes's neck "—step forward and confront your nemesis." When Orestes did not move, the man added, "Don't feel sorry for him, kid. He betrayed you."

Was there an element of compassion in his voice?

"Betrayed? How?"

The gloved hand crashed hard across his mouth, bringing blood to his lips.

"I ask the questions," the man said. "He drugged you. You should be high as a kite. Off your face. How sweet it is to watch the little children suffer."

Orestes clutched the knife with both hands so that it stuck out, like an erection, before him. He was so scared his entire body was shaking and covered in a sheen of sweat.

He took a step forward and instantly bumped into Sid; he must have been standing very close the whole time.

Hopefully, Orestes thought, *Sid is assessing the situation in that quick brain of his. He probably has a plan to get us out of this mess.*

The rope slackened between them.

"Is it true?" Orestes murmured. "What he said?"

Sid did not reply. Instead, he grabbed Orestes by the wrists and pulled him hard against his own body, so that they stood toe to toe, nose to nose, chest to chest. Sid gasped, let off a muffled groan, and expelled air between his teeth in a long painful hiss. Orestes hoped it was because they stood close together, for the first and possibly the final time.

When Sid spoke, his voice was shallow. "He told me to do it. Stuff in the Coke."

"That's why I'm wasted."

"I didn't know it was going to be like this. I swear."

Sid was making small, pained noises the whole time; he was having trouble speaking. If Orestes was not almost gone, he would have noticed.

"I thought I was safe with you."

Sid did not reply.

The man said, "Let the fight begin."

Orestes ignored him. "No problem," he said to Sid. "But I don't want to hurt you."

"You already have."

The man gasped.

That is when Orestes realized the knife was buried to the hilt in Sid's gut. It must have happened when Sid pulled him close. In his delirium and fear he had not noticed the blood pool at his feet, making the floor sticky, his toes warm. As the truth registered, Sid tightened the grip on Orestes's wrists and with a terrible cry dropped to his knees.

The knife unzipped him all the way to the chin, snagging bones along the way.

The word "No" shot out of Orestes's mouth. In it was all the fear, futility, and agony of his young life. His thighs and legs were doused with Sid's blood. He pulled the knife from the body and flailed with the weapon.

The nail gun went off in the man's hand.

The first nail whizzed inches past Orestes's ear.

The second nail lodged in his right shoulder.

Orestes screamed, swung blindly with the knife, and lodged it in a fleshy mass behind him.

The man's howls went unnoticed, as did Orestes's own rending attempts to dislodge the blade from whatever held it captive. He moved it up and down several times, twisting it around in an effort to set it free.

When he finally managed to get it out, he fell to his knees beside Sid, and began to work.

He was so delirious, he imagined himself kneeling on the floor, beneath a bright spotlight, as he prepared the means of his great escape from this terrible place.

First, he used the knife to deepen the incision from sternum to navel. Next, he pushed both hands into the cavity and pried it open. Entrails and organs spilled out. If he wasn't so wrecked, so deranged, he would have noticed that he was awash in blood, up to his elbows in guts. And he screamed the whole time. Screamed until his throat was raw and torn.

Although the room was pitch-black, in his mind's eye, in the depths of his sweeping delirium, he saw very clearly. What he perceived was a chest that contained nothing—no organs, no blood, no veins or tendons. Just an arch of bone that formed the ribs.

Sid was an empty husk, scrubbed clean of viscera and waiting.

Repeatedly, he told himself Sid hadn't betrayed him. If anything, he had readied his body for this eventuality— a boat to carry Orestes far from madness to safety.

It was the same with the arms and legs. They were hollow, vacant and waiting for a tenant to step into them, like a jacket or a new pair of trousers.

Sid was empty, waiting for Orestes to step inside and be transported. He had said he'd look after Orestes and he had remained true to his word. He was hollow. There was nothing to him. A shell, waiting to be filled.

Behind Orestes the tall man continued to wail and thrash on the floor. Then he, too, went quiet.

As dawn filtered around the edges of the cabin door, Orestes wedged himself under Sid's carved-out torso, imagined he fitted his arms into Sid's empty arms, and his legs in Sid's empty legs, and began to crawl toward the light, Sid's hacked cadaver hitching a ride on his back.

"You didn't let me down," Orestes said. "We're both safe."

Hours later the fleshy lid was taken off him. There was blinding light, sand, water. Hands, alarmed voices; he was lifted.

Chapter Three

WERRIBEE POLICE STATION
6:22 P.M. AUGUST 16, 1991

Doctor Sidawi emerged shaken from the interrogation room little over an hour later.

"You heard?"

Amanda Cribbe nodded and handed him strong black coffee in a paper cup.

"Can't thank you enough, Khaled." She patted him on the back.

"How did you find him?" Sidawi said, sipping the much-needed drink.

"Jackson's Cove. Dog walker reported a body in the sand. When our people moved the corpse, they found this little bastard under it. Literally. Looked like he'd tried to stuff himself in it." She shook her head in disbelief. "Gave the boys a hell of a scare."

"Was the corpse Sid's?"

"Yep. Real low-life." Cribbe consulted her notes. "Twenty-five. Drugs. Pimped young boys. Good businessman by the sounds."

"Come on, Amanda, spill the beans. What happened out there? You must know something."

She grimaced. "This is confidential."

Sidawi indicated his lips were sealed by pulling a make-believe zipper across his mouth.

"We found almost twenty-four bodies in two cabins. They were hanging from hooks. An injured party—a bald guy with a red beard—was found in one of the cabins. He's in a coma. Looks like a lawnmower ran over his face. A knife is being fingerprinted as we speak, and three suspects have been arrested."

"Suspects?"

"Yep. A tunnel at the back of a cabin leads to an underground chamber with industrial meat mincers and storage vats. It looks like people were being lured out there, killed, and turned into fertilizer for the vegetable gardens. They also had a nice line in snuff films. Melbourne's vegetarians are in for a shock, doc. It's like a factory for processing human beings.

"Are you all right? You look kinda pale." Cribbe tried to hide a smile.

Sidawi nodded. He had been until that moment a devout vegan.

"The scary thing is," Cribbe continued, "it looks like they had outside assistance."

"What do you mean?"

Cribbe cleared her throat and dropped her voice. "There's evidence members of the illustrious constabulary might be involved."

"Well, well..." Sidawi was not surprised. He liked Amanda but, as a Lebanese man living in the western suburbs, he harbored no illusions about the rest of the police force. He checked his watch. "Listen, I've an appointment. If there's nothing else..."

Amanda Cribbe shook her head and opened the outer door for him.

Sidawi stopped in the doorway and glanced at the boy.

"What's going to happen to him?"

Cribbe's face was serious. "Who knows? I mean look at him."

"Keep me posted, will you?"

"Are you taking an interest?" she said, smiling.

Sidawi gave a grim nod of the head, shrugged his shoulders.

"Thought you might," Cribbe added, the smile widening.

"He's going to need all the help he can get. Who knows what else is in his past?" Sidawi turned to leave and stopped again. "And clean him up, will you?"

This time he did leave because he really could not stand to look at the boy's face another moment.

Orestes Gallanos stood at the two-way mirror, nose pressed to the glass, bright eyes on Khaled Sidawi. The blanket lay on the floor, a cast-off skin, so that the red face, etched with hunger and yearning, seemed flayed of humanity. His mouth moved and the last thing the doctor heard through the crackly speaker was "Safe?"

THE LONG

LONELY ROAD

On a tiny island, in a forgotten corner of the north Aegean Sea, lived a boy. His name was Ali.

One fine morning he was dressing in his room. He and his mother were going to the country on an errand.

Ali bounded down the stairs, tucking his white shirt in his shorts. He sat on a stool and slipped on brown sandals, while his dog Olala frolicked at his feet.

"There you are," Ali's mother said. "Quick, get on the donkey. We've lots to do today."

At a mere four years old, Ali was too small to get on the donkey on his own. His mother had to help him, and she did this by hoisting him on to the saddle that was strapped to the animal's back. Two large wicker baskets called panniers hung either side of the saddle, grazing the backs of Ali's bare legs.

Off they went, clip-clop through the streets. It was eerily quiet. There was not a soul in sight.

The donkey's name was Locomotive. He was a skittish beast, always on the lookout for someone to bite with his big yellow teeth or kick with his flying hooves. It was said that he could outrun a train without trying.

Truth be told, Ali was scared of Locomotive. But he did not let on. He wanted his mother to think him brave; and his mother needed to believe that her son was brave, too, because Ali's father had died and they were alone in the world. The mother still grieved in the dead of night, quietly sobbing in her lonesome pillow. Yet Ali could barely remember the man's face.

On the road that leads out of town, they passed the primary school. Coming from inside, Ali heard students reciting lessons in clear, sparrow-like voices.

"When can I go to school?"

"You like learning, do you?"

The mother did not see her son nod because she was facing determinedly forward. Her sights were set on a very important mission which had to be completed that day.

"Don't be in a hurry to grow up," she said after a while. Her long dark hair was pulled back in a light-blue headscarf that fluttered at the nape of her neck.

They came to the edge of the village. The cobbles ended and the houses stopped. The narrow street turned into a dusty road that coiled to the horizon.

Ali's mother tugged the donkey's lead. "Come on, you, hurry up."

With one step, they entered the countryside. Olala trotted ahead, flushing birds out of the shrubbery.

Ali's mother had said they were going to the country house to clean up before moving to town for winter. But Ali was confused. They did that last week. *Maybe my mother has forgotten*, he thought, and contented himself with studying the bare hills that almost came down to nudge the edges of the road.

After a while, Ali grew uneasy. When he studied the back of his mother's head, it was almost as if he didn't know her. She had turned her back on him. As if she hated him. Didn't want him anymore. Of course, that couldn't be true. His mother loved him, and he loved her. And yet there was something wrong about her bearing. About the way she looked at him and the way her mouth was set, like a stubborn line drawn on the page.

At a fork in the road, they passed the smithy. It was an odd place and it fascinated Ali.

Aside from the high ringing sound of metal on metal, he loved the sparks that flew out of the door and two windows. He imagined that a dragon lived inside, crackling blazes in its sleep. The ramshackle building seemed to have fallen from the sky one stormy night, thrown together with scraps of wood, rock, metal, and bits of glass.

There were rumors about the man who lived there. Some said he was a djinni in charge of fire and dust. Others claimed he was the god Hephaestus, son of Zeus, come to earth to set up his divine forge. He was certainly ugly enough to pass for the gods' blacksmith. Looking at the strange tumbledown house, Ali believed it was all true and it made his small frame shiver with purest delight.

He eyed the yard enviously. It would be nice to play there one day. First, he needed to make friends with the blacksmith.

Ali's mother was not impressed. "What an eyesore," she grumbled. "What a din! Oh, my ears. Let's get out of here."

Olala barked, a high, shrill offering to the sky. That brought the blacksmith to the door. As Ali's grandmother liked to say, he was not the sort of man you want to meet in a dark alley. He was a giant of a man, eyes glinting out of a begrimed face. Red hair flamed from the crown of his head, stiff as the straw on a broomstick. As he stood there, filling the doorway with his huge frame, it looked like he was made of stone and fire. Master of all djinn.

The apprentice, a beanpole of a boy with coal-black hair and big dark eyes, peered out from behind the blacksmith.

Ali waved to them, but the men merely glared in his direction. The blacksmith muttered something. Then he pushed the apprentice inside and slammed the door.

Ali was crestfallen. There went his chances of making friends with them. He really wanted the men to acknowledge him. As if reading his mind, Olala dashed to the smithy and barked at the closed door.

"Get away from here, you cur," the man shouted from inside.

"Olala, come here at once," Ali's mother snapped.

The white terrier trotted back; ears flattened to her skull. Ali's mother put down her head and kept going.

Ali turned in the saddle and looked back at the smithy. "See you later," he called.

"Be quiet," his mother hissed. "Talking too much is a sin."

"Why?"

His mother shrugged. "I don't know. It's what they say."

From there on, they were in open country—the four of them, sliding between wedges of silence that slipped down from the hilltops to invade the valley. Fields, vineyards, orchards, and olive groves went on for miles, grazing the flinty shore where sea met sun-burnished soil. The sun rose high in the sky. It beat down like an anvil.

"Where's your hat?" Ali's mother said.

"I forgot to bring it."

The mother removed a yellow bandana from a cloth shoulder bag and tied a knot in each corner. She placed the makeshift hat on Ali's head.

"You don't want to get sunburned." She took hold of the donkey's reins and, with an encouraging word to Locomotive, set off again.

The sun rose higher. It was almost at its peak. And it burned, as hot as summer.

Ali was drowsy in the saddle. The sound of hooves on dusty road, the squeak of the swaying saddle, the back of his mother's head as she walked, moving from one leg to the other, the seesawing landscape, everything conspired to make him sleepy.

His eyes drooped. He tilted forward in his seat. And then he tilted sideways. Olala barked and Ali's head snapped back. His eyes flew open and he sat up straight. He had almost fallen asleep on the donkey's back. *That's dangerous. You could fall off and then what?*

After a while, Ali's eyes fluttered again. The swaying saddle reminded him of his mother singing a lullaby while he slept in the crib that swung back and forth, back and forth from two sturdy ropes tied to the wooden beams in the ceiling, when he was a baby. It seemed so long ago. Yet he remembered it as if it was yesterday.

His eyes closed and he slept. His body lolled from side to side and tilted dangerously forward.

As he slowly descended into the netherworld, Ali felt a pressure on his chest. It was as if someone had placed a rock on his chest. His lungs almost burst, and he struggled for breath. He thought he might suffocate, but by that stage he was well and truly asleep.

This time Olala did not bark. She was chasing skinks in the sunburned grass. And Ali's mother watched the road ahead, not her boy.

Ali's hands released their grip on the saddle handles and, without making a sound, he toppled off Locomotive's back.

Ali's mother said something about the fig trees in Uncle Atlas's property. When Ali did not respond, she turned to see why and froze to the spot. The saddle was empty. Her son had vanished.

She let out a horrified little gasp. Locomotive jerked his head, startled. Olala yipped and rushed over to see what was happening.

"Ali," the mother called. She ran hither and yon, searching the roadside.

There was no answer. Only silence and sky. Insects in the long grass.

Being more or less a young girl herself, she was frightened out of her wits. She tied Locomotive to an almond sapling and raced helter-skelter the way she came, calling her son's name and searching. She was sure Ali had fallen and was lying unconscious in a ditch.

After losing her husband, she couldn't afford to lose her son as well. What would people say? That she was careless, she supposed. And that she got what she deserved.

In this manner, she dashed more than halfway back to the village. The island echoed with her screams and lamentations. Everyone heard. Women poked their heads out of windows and men in fields stopped hoeing and straightened up their backs to get a better view. Dogs howled in backyards. Mules showed the whites of their eyes. But no one came to her aid. They knew better than to interfere.

Exhausted, Ali's mother collapsed on a rock by the roadside and started to cry. She was almost at the blacksmith's door.

Ali was gone. She might as well face it. Allah had seen fit to take him from her as well.

"Where could he be?" she wailed, throwing dust in the air and rubbing it in her hair and face.

Olala bounded beside her, yipping, thinking it was a game.

"Find him, you wretch." She pushed the dog away. "What good are you?"

Meanwhile, Ali woke up. He was squashed in an uncomfortable position, and his face was pressed against a hard, scratchy surface. Where could he be? He had trouble breathing. He gasped for air and tried to open his eyes. They were sticky as glue. His mouth tasted funny and he felt as if he rose to the surface from great oceanic depths known only to his fisherman father.

Then he heard his mother call from afar. She sounded faint, distant, as though her voice came from another world.

He opened his eyes and took a desperate gulp of air. His lungs almost burst. They hurt inside his ribcage. And for some reason, he was upside down, stuffed in a confined, narrow space. With difficulty, he managed to turn around and climbed to his feet. The top of his head popped out first, followed by his eyes. He was inside a basket. He had not fallen to the ground after all. He was inside one of the big wicker baskets on the donkey's back. If his mother had searched, she would have seen him immediately.

Ali looked around. His mother was gone. So was Olala. He was alone, inside a basket on Locomotive's back.

The animal glared at Ali with open hostility. Then he began to bray and tug at the reins. Thankfully, Ali's mother knew how to tie a strong knot.

Ali leaped out of the basket and scooted away from the flying hooves. Straightening the bandana-hat on his head, he looked around. "Mom?" he said, anxious and afraid.

There was no answer. He had to face facts. For some reason, his mother had abandoned him in the wild, like the children in fairy stories left to fend for themselves in wolf-haunted forests. And like the children in fairy stories, he knew he had to prove himself by making his way home. He could walk, but he didn't want to leave Locomotive. Someone might come along and steal him.

Ali had an idea. This was a test. Even though he was terrified of Locomotive, he had to gather his courage and ride the animal home. That way his mother would know of her son's bravery and she would never leave him alone again.

He checked his pockets for an apple or a carrot with which to bribe the animal. There was nothing. The almond tree was bare.

All right, Ali thought, *I have to rely on my wits.*

He took a deep breath and faced Locomotive. They eyed each other with great suspicion and mistrust, the animal and the boy.

After many failed attempts, falls and scuffles in the dust, Ali managed to clamber on Locomotive's back. It was not easy. First, he had to stand on a fallen branch while the donkey shimmied and skittered away and tried to bite with big yellow teeth.

When Ali was finally in the saddle, he grabbed the handles and held on. Then he leaned forward and carefully untied the reins around the sapling.

Locomotive bolted as if he had been shot out of a cannon, madly bucking and braying, all the way back to town.

Ali held on for dear life, his eyes shut tight and his mouth open in a high-pitched wail.

Ali's mother heard. She leaped to her feet. It sounded as if her son's voice had fallen from the sky. Surely, he wasn't calling from heaven. Then she heard the shrill cry again. It came from a distance to be sure, but it was definitely on solid ground. Not paradise.

Drying her tears, she pulled herself together and raced in the direction of Ali's voice.

In no time, she was confronted by a huge dust cloud. It gathered force and sped her way, covering the road from one side to other as it twisted and turned, like water boiling furiously in a pot. She froze to the spot, mystified. What could it be? And what was the noise coming from inside?

A scream. Her horror doubled. A djinni had Ali in his clutches, for sure. She ran faster, her arms outspread as though to embrace the world and undo the undoable. She would do anything to save her little boy and she was mightily sorry for leaving him alone.

The dust cloud and the woman raced toward each other from opposite ends of the road. As they came closer, she saw frightening, bewildering shapes moving inside. It was a vision from hell, a terrible djinni with many limbs and wings emitting unearthly cries from a huge jagged maw. She knew without a doubt that it had come to punish her for her sins.

When the dust cloud was almost upon Ali's mother, her courage failed. She hesitated and stepped aside. In that instant, the cloud swirled by in a pandemonium.

Seconds before she closed her eyes to stop dust from getting in them, she saw Ali go past at speed, raised several feet from the ground.

"Maaaaaaa," he wailed.

"He-haw, he-haw, he-haw," brayed Locomotive.

It was not a djinni at all. It was her boy on the donkey's back. She cursed herself for her folly and raced after them. But she didn't stand a chance. Locomotive was too fast. Try as she might, she couldn't catch up.

As if the sight of Ali clinging to the back of a crazed animal was not enough, she was now confronted by a far worse vision.

A giant with flaming red hair appeared out of the maelstrom and ran toward her boy. The ifrit, for surely that's what it was, held a green plant in his hand; and, as he charged at Locomotive, he flicked his thick hairy wrist and released a spray of water from the glistening leaves.

The droplets of water flew through the air in slow motion, each bead a sparkling world with a rainbow inside it.

One and then two beads of water hit Locomotive on the forehead. The donkey howled and skidded to a halt.

Ali froze on the animal's back, eyes wide open.

The ifrit with the red hair was the blacksmith, half naked and grimy with soot. Nonetheless, he was fearsome as a demon as he dipped a sprig of fragrant basil in a jar of water and sprayed it over the scene, shouting prayers in a loud voice.

Ali said, "Why are you doing that?"

Summing up the last of her strength, Ali's mother ran up, scooped the boy in her arms, and backed away from the blacksmith.

"Leave us alone," she yelled.

"Go back to hell," the blacksmith called back. "Leave this town in peace."

He dipped the basil in the jar and flung more water on Ali's mother. Some of it hit Ali's cheek. It burned, causing his skin to flake and peel back to the bone. But he felt no pain.

Ali's mother stared at the man in mute horror. "Please..." she managed.

"Be gone, devil," the blacksmith cried.

"Have pity," the mother cried, but already Ali felt an enervating coldness in his bones. In seconds he was transparently blue and fading fast as mist in the morning sun, so that the light passed through him and fell on the stones visible through his mother's glassy feet. Locomotive turned to gray gauze and faded with a faint bray. There was a loud bang. Like thunder. It came from nowhere. His mother's head bloomed into a large crimson flower, a hibiscus or an iris, and lashed insanely from side to side. It wavered on the stalk of her shattered neck before blowing away in a light breeze. Her arms did not release Ali so much as simply ceased to hold him. She stepped back and was no more.

Floating a few feet above the ground, Ali had time to lock eyes with the blacksmith before he too vanished. In the instant before all sight ended for him, he found himself atop a rocky crag, looking down the hillside to the bluest sea imaginable. A stocky man waved to him from a fishing vessel with a sail.

Then that too faded and Ali was gone.

Olala came to sniff the ground at the blacksmith's feet. He stamped his foot and cursed. "Dirty, unclean cur."

The dog tucked her tail between her legs and scooted away.

"What in the name of the prophet, blessed be his name, was that?" cried the apprentice. His body trembled inside the threadbare clothes, despite the heat of the day.

The blacksmith said, "It's a sad story, lad. Happened years ago, before you came to this accursed village for your apprenticeship..."

"But what was it, uncle?" the boy persisted. "Those things. Were they ghouls?"

The blacksmith shook his head. "Ghosts," he said.

The apprentice muttered a prayer under his breath and said, "Ghosts, in daylight?"

"The mother went mad after her husband drowned at sea," the blacksmith continued. "She took her son out to the country house and smothered him with a pillow. Then she pretended bandits kidnapped him. The police found the poor boy a day or so later. He'd been stuffed in one of those baskets you put on a donkey. When they came for the mother, she shot the donkey with a shotgun and blew her own head off. Heaven knows how the dog escaped." The blacksmith shook his head before adding, "Her name was Ebru. The boy was Ali. He would have been about nine years old now if he lived."

The man cast a wary eye at Olala. The white terrier crouched under a carob tree and watched him speak the familiar names: Ali, Ebru. Yes, she knew the names well. They were burned in her memory. There was a time when either one of those names spoken aloud would have caused her purest delight. She would have shot to her feet and come running. But the owners of the names were gone. They returned once a year for a brief visit, before going back to wherever they came from.

"That cursed dog knows when they're coming back," the blacksmith went on. "She alerted me to their presence this morning. When she went past, I knew we were in for a hell of a day. So, I armed myself with holy water from the Zamzam well. It wards off evil spirits, you know."

"Will they come back?"

"Every year on this day," the older man replied, letting the basil slip from his fingers to the ground. "Like clockwork." He laid a hand on the boy's shoulder. "Let's get back to work. We've lots to do today."

The blacksmith and his apprentice went back to the smithy. The basil sprig wilted in the sun. A westerly wind swept the road, causing a faint spiral of dust to rise in the midday sun and dance along the road as it coiled toward the higgledy-piggledy building, there to break against the stone fence.

After a while, Olala came out from under the carob tree and made her way to the ruined windmill on the hill, there to wait for that glorious day—a full year away—when Ali, Ebru, and yes, even grumpy old Locomotive would come calling her name.

"Olala, where are you? Olala, come quick. We're going to the country."

LIGHT IN HER EYES

"A day or two in the country will do you good." Her mother's words echoed in Mila's mind. "Are you sure you don't want me to come?"

Mila was definite. "No, Mom. I need time for myself. I'll call when I get there." That was two hours ago. *From Newstead*, the email printout from Miss Lake read, *turn left on to the Daylesford-Newstead Road and then turn on to the Creswick-Newstead Road. Go through Providence Gully. Turn left into Honeybone Lane and it's the second cottage on the right. Key in meter box at back door.* And that's exactly what Mila had done, after stopping for a coffee at the Lost Angels Cafe in Newstead. Now the tree-lined road coiled before her, going up and down inclines, twisting and turning as shadows piled on the ground ahead of the red Mini and dispersed when the sun peeked from behind billowing clouds that filled the sky like an arriving wave.

It was a blustery late summer's day, with a tearing wind that bent trees and grasses to one side so the leaves showed white undersides and crows were tossed in the air like scraps of crepe paper.

Mila took her time. It was twelve-thirty in the afternoon and there was no hurry. She had rented the house for two nights. She could do as her heart desired. After everything she had been through that week, it was a relief.

She had not seen another car in several minutes. Yellow fields stretched on either side. Hills rose and fell and once or twice the hatchback traversed a bridge that dashed over a gully with a dry creek bed among tossing reeds. Light shifted through thick stands of trees to reveal high green countryside on one side and changed again to cast the same landscape into a gloomy aspect. She rolled down the window and breathed the warm, fragrant air. She removed a dark strand from her mouth and adjusted her sunglasses. A blue van appeared in the rear-view mirror and for a moment her heart almost stopped.

It's Paul, she thought. *He followed me.*

And then she realized it was not his car. When the road straightened, the vehicle overtook her and disappeared around a bend, an older man behind the wheel. Relieved, she sighed and tried to get back in the mood.

It was a day for new beginnings. Like the tight bud of a rose, her heart opened to greet the world and nature's sweet promise. The tank was full; if she wanted, she could keep driving and never stop, or at least not for a while. Never go back to her old life, her stuffy flat, to the breakup with Paul, to the knowledge of what she had done. Go someplace where no one knew her, settle down, get a job at a local newspaper and take photographs...

She passed a wooden church high on a hilltop and crossed herself. Almost immediately after that, she spotted the sign for Honeybone Lane and had to quickly apply the brake before she shot past the turnoff. Daydreams of a new life were nipped in the bud. But she noted with no small amount of relief that a farmhouse was nearby if she needed anything over the next couple of days; it wasn't ideal for a woman to be alone in the country.

The narrow unsealed lane led to a miner's cottage on a circular gravel drive, box-ironbark forest on the other side of a yellow paddock. Fighting off shooting pains in the hips and inner thighs, she removed a small wheeled-suitcase from the trunk, and rattled across the brick courtyard to the back door. As promised, the key was in the meter box. She walked with it to the front of the house, marveling at how trusting country people were. Up three steps to the verandah festooned with pink briar roses. Peppercorn trees hissed and thrashed in the wind as she unlocked the door and pushed it open.

Cool air hit her first. Then came the dry musty smell of a place locked up for too long. After the day's bright light, it was dark inside. She allowed her eyes to adjust before stepping over the threshold. The moment she stood in the hallway, the wind ceased to shout. Stillness dropped over everything. It was a relief. She put down the suitcase, breathed in the air, and knew she had made the right decision to come alone. It would do her spirits good, even if the solitude encouraged unwanted thoughts.

It was then she heard a faint rustle. She listened. It came from further down the passage, in the room beyond. In the light coming through the front door, she made out a collection of furniture. It was only when her eyes adjusted to the lusterless light falling on the floor that she perceived something immediately in the doorway. It flashed behind an armchair with the speed of a rodent. She started and then laughed at herself.

"It's a bush mouse, you idiot," she said, though it was an unusually pale mouse, and bigger than expected. "These houses are full of them. Probably have snakes in the ceiling too."

Just as well she wasn't squeamish.

The sitting room at the end of the hall was equipped with a small television, a primitive sound system, a lumpy couch with cushions, two armchairs, and a wood heater. Not that she'd be using the latter; it was so warm. She pulled up the blind over the single sash window and let in light. There was no sign of the mouse, just a very still huntsman spider beside a picture on the wall. She continued to explore. A small dining room led off the sitting room and opened on a narrow passage with a bathroom and kitchen at the back.

Feeling agitated, she decided to have a drink before settling in. She left the bags in the hallway, returned to the car via the back door, and carried two cardboard boxes to the kitchen. One contained food, the other alcohol. Cracking open a bottle, she poured a liberal amount of red wine into a green glass goblet and threw it back in one go. When she felt its coruscating warmth in her gut, she poured a second glass and, taking it to the front porch, settled with a sigh in a nice deep cane chair.

Fruit trees surrounded a sedate garden of roses and lavender, keeping at bay the towering gray trees in the forest. Sighing again, feeling her shoulders relax for the first time in days, she picked up the glass and drank. Feeling light-headed—she really should have brought crackers and cheese—she closed her eyes and breathed in the fresh smells of dry grass and eucalyptus.

Her eyes flew open as if on a summons from a crow's call. And unexpectedly, for she hadn't been thinking of anything, tears spilled down her face. She sat hunched over for some time, weeping in her hands, and letting out the accumulated stress of the week.

"What have I done?" she said. "Oh, God, what have I done? Please forgive me."

She dabbed her eyes with a handkerchief, blew her nose, and drained the glass. After a while, she retrieved the open bottle from the kitchen and, over the next half hour, proceeded to finish it, dozing on and off in the chair as the wind picked up and clouds sped over the cottage.

Everything will be all right, she told herself, finally. *It's behind you now. You're here to relax and begin a new life.*

Determined to pull herself together, she stood on wobbly legs and headed indoors. Time to decide which room she was going to occupy and maybe go for a walk in the forest afterward.

Standing in the hall, she stuck her head in the room on the right. Double bed, old-fashioned timber bureau with dried lavender in a white vase, wardrobe, and a window with a frayed blind. The room to the left was slightly smaller, with a vaulted wooden ceiling, a double bed, an old-fashioned dressing table and a narrow wardrobe next to the window with the pulled-down blind. It was the cast-iron fireplace with the bright-red tiles that won the day. She was not likely to use it in this heat but it would be nice to look at it. It fulfilled a fantasy of quaint weekend getaways, with lavender satchels under pillows, quilts, and fluffy white towels.

Mila picked up the suitcase and went to enter the room. It was then she realized she had mistakenly turned one too many times, perhaps. For now, she was headed into the other room, the one on the right. She turned again, only to see the very same room—the unwanted one—yet again. With all the wine and the subdued light, she had become confused, dizzy. She really needed some food in her stomach. She tried yet again but her efforts were always frustrated; she couldn't enter the correct room.

Despite the open front door, the air was close. She mopped her forehead with the back of her hand, brushed hair out of her eyes. Then she picked up the suitcase again, this time determined to get in. As she stepped forward, she tripped over the rug and pitched to the side, knocking her elbow on the stone wall. It hurt. The suitcase dropped from her hand with a clatter. She steadied herself against the cool stone and, for the third time, found herself still turned the other way.

"What's going on?" she said aloud. The thickness of the walls absorbed her voice, muffling it. She inspected her elbow, licked a finger, and rubbed spittle on the graze, thinking *this is not exactly an auspicious beginning.*

From a distance, a sound came to her: children singing, which surprised and pleased her in equal measure.

Must be the farmer's children, come to greet me, she thought.

The absurdity of the thought struck her soon after and she laughed. *Children don't go around greeting strangers with song and dance,* she thought. *This is not a story book.* And yet it continued. A gentle sighing that rose and fell with mournful modulation and seemed to come from the building itself. Not from outside. It held, too, a strange muttering, like a lullaby, soothing one moment, sad the next.

She spun quickly and tripped over the suitcase. The breath was knocked out of her and she lay face down on the floor, aching, muttering curses.

That's when she realized the voices came from the bedroom on the left.

She shook her head and thought, *Okay, you've had way too much to drink.*

There came a slight noise—a grating of metal—and quiet fell.

Rattled, she rose to her feet and crept forward, peering anxiously into the room. She wasn't the type to back off easily; it was not how her mother raised her: "Look after yourself, kid. Because no one else is going to do it for you." It was empty, of course. How could it be otherwise? There was only the inviting bed, the bedside tables with lamps on either side.

Only now the back flap was open in the fireplace and sitting in the grate was a teddy bear.

You were not there before, she thought. *I would have noticed you.*

She entered with no trouble at all this time, picked up the toy, and turned it over. It was a rough homemade affair of white knitted wool with bright-pink ears and black smudges for eyes, nose, and mouth. The front was gray with soot and damp. She pictured an expectant mother knitting it for her baby and taking great care with the detail.

"You must have fallen down the chimney. How strange. How long have you been up there?" Mila said aloud, dusting it with her fingers and making things worse in the process. Still holding the bear, she knelt on the hearth and looked up the flue. Nothing there. "Well, Sooty," she said, standing. "I'd like to know who put you up there and why."

She placed Sooty on the bed, brought in her suitcase, and arranged her things in the cupboard and on the dressing table. The room seemed to have lost the desire to keep her out. Or maybe she had been drunk and tripping over her own feet. She never could hold her liquor, while Paul drank till the cows came home.

In the small, neat bathroom, she inspected her underwear for the spotting that had plagued her for the last four days and found that it persisted. She showered carefully, changed into fresh clothes, and went for a stroll along the lane as the sun dipped behind the trees, casting long shadows on the ground.

*

The walk did her good. She returned an hour or so later, refreshed and clear-headed. She shucked off her walking boots, opened another bottle of red, and took the glass out to the porch along with her cell phone.

She dialed her mother's number.

"Galea, it's me," she said, addressing her mother by her first name.

"Thank God. I was worried."

Mila chuckled. "I went to the country, Mom. Not another country."

"Are you all right?" Galea said. "Is the house nice?"

"It's paradise. I love it."

There was a pause at the other end. "How are you?"

There were no secrets between mother and daughter. "Yeah, good..." Mila ventured.

"But..."

"I'm having those 'emotional reactions' the doctor predicted."

"You chose to get rid of the baby," Galea stated, direct as ever. "No one forced you."

In other words, if you feel guilty, it's your fault. Mila didn't take offense; she knew her mother well enough to know her reaction came from a tough-love kind of place. Face things and move on was her mother's motto. Don't wallow.

"Oh, Mom," she said, the tears welling up again. "I think I made a terrible mistake."

"Thought you might change your mind."

"If I could take it back, I would," Mila went on.

"It's a sin to kill an unborn baby. I told you to keep it and I'd help you look after it. But you never listen."

She almost wailed into the phone. "Fuck sin, Mom. I wanted to cut ties with Paul. Not get rid of the baby. I'd be tied to him for the rest of my life if I had his child."

"You should have thought of that before getting pregnant with him."

Sometimes, Mila thought, *Galea can be a little too hardboiled.* She sighed and decided to drop the subject.

"It wasn't really a baby yet," she said. "First trimester and all that stuff."

She sipped more wine and wished she had brought cigarettes with her, having given up when she still entertained the idea of keeping the child. She had even gone out and bought toys and plastic feeding bowls, picturing cozy nursery scenes and music boxes.

"Every life is precious in the Lord's eyes," Galea replied. "You committed a great sin and now you must face up to it."

"Listen, gotta go," Mila replied. "See you Sunday afternoon." She was not yet ready to dwell on sin and atonement.

"Call if you need anything."

"Don't worry. I've neighbors down the lane. They seem nice. They even waved at me from their cute ivy-covered cottage when I drove past."

She had no idea why she added that fantasy. Probably to reassure her mother.

Mila ventured to the kitchen to arm herself with another glass of wine before tackling a meal—not her strong point at the best of times. Another reason why she and Paul fought. He expected her to do the cooking and she did not see why she should. It would be pasta, pasta, and pasta for the next two days. Out of the box.

She made her way back to the porch.

The front of the house faced due west so that as the sun dipped lower on the horizon, it washed the facade with the day's last light. Mila was in the corridor, facing the entrance, when a shadow fell on the floor in front of her. It extended from the door to her sneaker-clad feet. Startled, she gasped and looked up. The wineglass slipped from her hands and shattered on the floor.

A woman in a long black dress and hair pulled back from her face stood on the other side of the closed fly screen, head bowed, hands clasped before her.

"Hello, you must be Miss Lake," Mila said, thinking it was the owner of the cottage. "Sorry, you startled me—" and she stopped dead because there was no woman. Just a collection of light and shadow from the pitch and heave of foliage, falling on the ragtag collection of outdoor furniture. Yet the shadow remained in the hall. Mila clearly made out the head (it almost touched her toes), the shoulders, and the elongated trunk. She stepped back to readjust her vision, but the light refused to cooperate with the leaves and recreate the vision. Yet it's strange how the mind works. Mila was certain the woman had looked up and spoken. The words rang in her mind.

"Welcome to Briar Cottage, my dear." Then the shadow turned and walked away.

At this point a sensible person would pack and head for the car. But Mila was not the type. Her feet were firmly planted on the ground, and she knew emotional upheavals and mental aberrations were common for a woman who had undergone the kind of trial she had on Monday.

It's not easy aborting a child, even when the decision is yours. It was the suction that preyed on her mind most. A machine vacuuming her insides, scraping the uterus and taking life away as though it was the morning's garbage. She took no comfort in the knowledge that if Paul knew what she had done to their baby, he'd strangle her. Which is why Mila had not told him about the pregnancy, and why she had walked away from the three-year relationship. She couldn't live with a man who used her as a punching bag when he had one too many.

Feeling rattled but not wanting to let this ruin her holiday, she stuck her head out of the door and peered the length of the porch. No one. The garden remained as empty as it had been all along.

She cleaned up the broken glass and headed to the kitchen to dump it in the rubbish bin. On the way she turned on all the lights, from the front to the back of the house, put water on the boil for ravioli. It was as she passed the small alcove between kitchen and bathroom that she spotted the Guest Book beside the old-fashioned telephone. She settled with it on the porch with a glass of water—a rest from the red; she really was getting unsettled. Two mosquito repellents emitted acrid aromas beside her.

According to the potted history in the front of the volume, the cottage was built by Irishman Marc McBride in 1887. He lived there with his young wife, Sofie McBride, a healer. The next page contained a faded black-and-white photograph depicting the couple, a handsome man and a striking woman in a simple black dress and white collar. Her oval face contained a wide sensuous mouth, determined eyes, and light-colored hair pulled back on the broad forehead. Despite the poor-quality reproduction, Mila recognized her immediately. It was, without a doubt, the same woman she saw earlier.

This is seriously freaking me out, she thought.

How could this be? She had never been in this house before and she had never looked inside this book until that moment. And yet she had seen Sofie McBride—a woman who died a very long time ago—stand outside this door.

Fear and dread of the unknown welled up inside Mila. Her first instinct was to get out of there. Fast. But that's not how she had been raised. She had been taught by Galea to stand her ground and work things out. Not run like a frightened chicken. Even so, there was no explaining this. It made no sense. And her mind could not entertain the obvious. That she had seen a ghost. That the place was haunted. It was absurd. She could not go there.

She was being silly. There must be a photo in the house, on one of the walls, though she couldn't think where. She must have seen it when she arrived, not taken any notice...and she had been drinking a lot. She was stressed, suggestible.

She gulped the water, took several deep breaths, and gazed at the garden.

Dusk was her favorite time. The subtle light hid more than it revealed. The pensive quiet of the land as day turned to night. The damp smells of earth. Now the wind had dropped, her ears picked up faint traffic sounds from far away. They indicated a world in a hurry, removed from her own leisurely circumstances.

When the sun finally dropped, Mila went inside. She boiled ravioli, zapped a satchel of bolognese in the antiquated microwave, and settled at the kitchen table with another glass of wine to savor the quiet.

The car arrived just as she finished her meal. First came the sound of an approaching engine. Then the courtyard outside the windows blazed with the sweep of headlights. Again, she thought immediately of Paul. He had found out about the abortion and he had come to beat the crap out of her for killing his child.

Heart pounding, she rose to her feet and stood behind the closed back door, which led directly onto the courtyard. Her hand moved to make sure it was locked. Even though it was not very sturdy. Paul was strong. A kick could bring it down. It occurred to her that the front door was closed but not locked. But it was too late to do anything about that.

Footsteps approached. Someone knocked.

"Hello," a woman's voice said.

"Who is it?"

"It's me, Miss Lake. The owner of the house, love. I'm sorry to bother you so late but—"

The door flew open so fast the woman on the other side leaped back in alarm. Mila stood on the threshold staring with open relief at a short middle-aged woman in brown corduroy pants and a blue checked shirt. Her long gray hair was pulled back in a ponytail. Lively pale-blue eyes sparked in the hesitantly smiling face.

"Are you all right?" Miss Lake said, looking at Mila with concern.

It took a while for Mila to reassure the woman.

"Please come in. I've had a bit of a week, that's all."

Mila pointed at a chair in the kitchen.

Miss Lake refused to take a seat. "I don't want to bother you. I just wanted to bring you these eggs from our chickens and a homemade pot of yogurt for your breakfast," she said. "I should have done it earlier, but it's been such a day, you wouldn't believe it…"

She held out a wicker basket. Mila took it and put it on the table, not sure what culinary delights she could whip up with the fresh produce. Maybe take it home and give them to her mother.

"I won't keep you," Miss Lake said, turning to leave. "Welcome to Briar Cottage and if you need anything, we're just down the road." She indicated the next house along the lane.

Mila had a thought. "Briar Cottage," she said. "That's a nice name for an interesting house."

"I see you've been reading its history," Miss Lake said, eyes falling on the Guest Book beside Mila's empty bowl.

"What sort of a healer was Sophie McBride?" Mila pursued the subject. "What did she do exactly?"

"She was a fascinating woman," Miss Lake said, leaning against the pantry door. "From what I gather, she was trained in traditional Irish home remedies, which she supplemented with local Aboriginal healing methods. She was a bit of a go-to woman for women in the district. Real doctors being scarce in those days."

Mila could see Miss Lake warm to the subject. Folding her arms across her chest, she sat on the edge of the table and listened with interest, her earlier frights almost forgotten.

"What's less well-known," Miss Lake continued in lower tones, "is that Mrs. McBride helped women end unwanted pregnancies."

Mila thought her heart would stop. Though she didn't know why she was surprised. Unwanted pregnancy was an eternal female fear. "She was an abortionist?"

Miss Lake nodded knowingly.

"How do you know?"

"Her diaries. Found them in the chimney of the bedroom with the vaulted ceiling when my partner, Amanda, and I renovated the place."

Mila's eyes shot in the direction of the room. "That's where I'm sleeping," she said.

"If you're interested, you can see the actual documents at the local historical society in town."

"I might just do that," Mila said.

"I'll be off," Miss Lake said. "I've bothered you long enough."

It was as Mila walked Miss Lake to the car that she thought to ask a niggly question.

"What happened to the McBrides?"

"Marc McBride died at a ripe old age, in this house," Miss Lake said, stopping in front of her car. "Sofie McBride passed away in Melbourne Gaol in 1900."

"Jail? What for?"

Miss Lake shrugged. "The abominable crime of assisting in abortion, of course."

After the woman left, Mila half watched a forgettable movie on DVD and then got ready for bed, knowing full well that night ruled on the other side of the flimsy panes of glass. Just to show she was not afraid, she stood in the pitch-black garden for several minutes and stared at the stars. Cold and uncaring. So very far away. So brilliant and yet so utterly dead.

It was only when she had climbed into bed with Sooty in her arms that she voiced what had been on her mind all along.

"What do you know?" she said to the bear. "An abortionist lived in this house. *Quelle coincidence.* Did Sofie McBride put you in the chimbley together with her diary, Mr. Sooty?" She paused. "And why didn't they find you when they found the diary?"

The teddy bear was not telling. He stared through an eyepatch of soot. Mila rubbed one of his pink ears and smiled. She pictured in her mind's eye the daily activities, possibly in this room. Women came to see Sofie McBride, some frightened, others hopeful, about ailments for which only the Irishwoman had knowledge, preparing medicines and ointments from plants found in the bush. And occasionally a young lass came to tell Sofie McBride a familiar tale of woe. A beau, a kiss that lead to more serious activity, and before too long a pregnancy that could not possibly see full term. By all accounts, Sofie McBride was willing to lend a hand and be silent thereafter about the clandestine activities conducted in this isolated hamlet, far from prying eyes. Others were not. And that's probably what landed her in prison.

"The secret life of houses," Mila said, holding the bear to her and soiling the white T-shirt she wore to bed. She touched its fleck of a nose and said, "Tell me, Mr. Sooty, what did Mrs. McBride do with the unwanted fetuses? Did she bury them in the garden to feed her plants? Under the floorboards? Did she stuff them up the chimbley to keep you company?"

The bear kept his own counsel.

"I understand," she said, dusting off her T-shirt and noting that a faint stain remained. "You're a discreet bear. You don't gossip."

A vision came to her of long-forgotten lives, with their little dramas, important one day, forgotten the next. Onto that interposed an unbidden foresight of the vast, tumultuous night as it lay thick on the land. In her isolation, she saw the cottage from high above. Way down there it was, on the edge of the bush. And in the creeping black there was only the wan glimmer from her window, a warning to some, an invitation to others. Blackness swooped down from the sky, like a bird of prey, passed through walls and prowled the corridors until it stood on the other side of the closed bedroom door, ready to knock and ask for an admittance whose only condition was a denial of light.

She felt it then. The lamp flickered beside the bed. And although the light remained on, the room went dark. Something within its walls turned to watch her. She pricked up her ears and listened, allowed her imagination to rove in the attic, under the floorboards, and outside where moonlight fell on stiff, glistening leaves.

She rolled her eyes, told herself to cool it. Stretching out under the covers, she cuddled Sooty before switching off the light. The room plunged into total darkness. There was only the comfort of the bear. Her eyes closed and there was the sensation of plunging headlong into sleep.

*

She sat up and realized there was faint light in the room. In the distance children sang a mournful lullaby. She stepped out of bed, kneeled in front of the fireplace in her T-shirt and knickers, and looked up the chimney. Rough stone steps went up until they disappeared. Way above, faint light beckoned and she thought she saw a pale face look down, curiosity mingled with fear. Or maybe it was several small faces, gazing through banisters. They ran off, giggling when they caught her eye.

She was dreaming, she had to be, but there was only one thing to do. Go and see what the children were up to. *Who are they? What do they want, singing and running away like that?*

Reaching up with both hands, she pulled herself into the flue and began to climb the stairs. It was easy. But there was a long way to go. There was no end to the grime and grit beneath her bare toes and fingers as she placed one foot in front of the other. One hand before the other. She passed an empty bird's nest, a rat's skeleton, white and gleaming amid the powdery black, and a doll's head without eyes. Thick cobwebs fluttered in corners where bricks jutted and acted as handholds when needed.

Just as it seemed the stairs would never end, her head came up through a hole in the floor.

A corridor stretched before her. It was lined with dozens of closed doors on either side. From behind each one she heard children hold their breath and wait for her to make the first move. She climbed out and began to walk. Yet each time she opened a door, she was greeted by swarming black. Or perhaps there was the feeling that someone had recently vacated the space, quickly scampering away.

A clock ticked in the distance. *Tick-tock. Tick-tock.* And as she moved along, she became aware of sobbing. A keening weeping that would not stop. It was a woman.

Each time she looked back at the ground she had covered, she saw children no bigger than the palm of her hand pressed hard against the plaster and following her stealthily from the shadows. She kneeled and opened her arms.

"Come to me," she said, becoming aware for the first time that Sooty was in her left hand. Except he was now clean. "Look," she said, holding him out. "Is he yours? Come get him."

A small hand darted out of the gloaming and snatched away Sooty. But no one stepped forward.

The clock ticked away. *Tick-tock. Tick-tock.* Except now it sounded more like a heartbeat. *Boom-boom. Boom-boom.*

She rose to her feet and continued. Eventually, she came to an open door. Sobbing came from inside a black room.

Mila stood where she was, hand on the doorjamb, and strained her eyes, hoping to catch a glimpse of whoever it was that wept so fretfully. She could not see a thing. There was only weeping, a solid uncompromising reality.

"Who are you?" she said. "What do you want?"

The sobbing stopped as though it had been cut off with scissors. A match flared. A candle was lit, far back, away from the door, near a window with thick colorless drapes. Mila advanced toward the light. She was connected to it by a long fibrous cord that reached from the candle to her navel. The children pressed in behind her, dozens, like a train on a swarming bridal gown. She paid them no heed. Her attention was on a small table with a burning candle.

The weeping woman was not there. But when Mila brought her right hand to the wood grain on the table a teardrop attached itself to the skin of her middle finger. She brought it to her lips, like a pearl, a sacrament, that tasted like clear mountain water in her mouth.

The heart stopped beating. *Boom-boom. Boom—*

She turned to face the children. "Time to go home," she said, weary at last.

No sooner were the words out of her mouth, than a great sound rang through the house. A deafening roar. Her ears ached. Her head throbbed. It was inside the walls, the doors, the ceiling, the floorboards. Inside her.

A sound like a furious, shrieking wind filled the house. The children were sucked backward, right out of the door and vanished. She was alone and she knew if she did not get out, she would be lost too. Summoning all the strength and courage in her body, she ran as fast as she could back the way she came.

All the doors were open now, to the left and to the right, and as she ran she caught a glimpse of every room along the way. There was nothing in them except an unending whiteness. The corridor was the only solid reality. That and the whirling suction. The wind that rushed after her, pulling her back.

Once she looked over her shoulder and saw that the hallway had disappeared. It had been eaten away. Perhaps by the gale. Or her own desperate tread. There was only a bleached nothingness.

Finally, she was at the trapdoor. Without thinking, she leaped. Fell into a void. Down she went. Into her bed.

*

She sat up in bed and saw that it was almost dawn. Faint light crept around the blind, a bird sang in the garden, and she became aware that she still cradled Sooty in her arms. He had not been left behind. She turned her attention to him and at first did not understand. Did not know if she ought to scream or smile.

She held a pulpy white thing. It was coiled in on itself, with a large distended forehead and bulging purple eyes covered over by a thin layer of transparent skin. It moved its limbs in jerks and starts in her arms, the orbs moving with stealth beneath black slits that had yet to form a proper eye. There was no mouth and two holes in the would-be face awaited the arrival of a nose. A part of her recoiled with horror. Another warmed to the creature, wanting to protect and shelter.

A second bird sang and a ray of sunlight came into the room from under the blind. Briefly, light swept away dark and she saw that the bed was covered with them. The creatures swarmed. They were everywhere. Almost piled on top of each other, squirming like slugs or worms. They were on the sheet she had used to cover herself during the night. On the pillows beside her head. In her lap. Pressed up close the length of her body. Writhing tiny things turned in on themselves, like snails without shells, with closed eyes and bunched-up hands pressed to the chest. All thrust up against her, wanting warmth, protection.

Fear turned to ecstasy. She was glad. Overjoyed. They had followed her after all. They were not back there with the sucking wind that would carry them away, into oblivion.

Another bird flew past the window, briefly blocking the early morning light. The room was semi-dark again and the bed contained only her solitary self. Even Sooty was gone. She almost wept.

The bedroom door swung open on well-oiled hinges. On the other side was the woman in black. She glided in on feet that did not move and stood at the foot of the bed. Briefly, she glanced up and their eyes met. An understanding passed between women.

"The Lord taketh away and the Lord giveth," Sophie McBride said.

She placed something under the thin white sheet that covered Mila.

In the depths of her misery Mila saw it move beneath the covers, making its way slowly, imperceptibly, from the foot of the bed to the center, keeping a firm aim between her legs. She lay back on the pillows and, lifting it, peered under the sheet.

It was a kind of pink leguminous pod with a swollen head, barely formed eyes and ears, the intimation of a tail and differentiated arms and legs pressed together around an umbilical cord that barely hid developing male genitalia.

"Are you my mother?" it said.

"My baby," Mila cried, aware that its voice was in her head. "I'm sorry I left you. And I'm so glad you came back."

She looked up to see the woman disappear into the passage. Then she turned her attention to the fetus.

"Come," she said. "Come to me."

She spread her legs further, an enticement the little bean did not ignore. Like a blind slug, it wriggled across the vast terrain of the bed, between soaring fleshy summits, rifts and gaps, toward a dripping forested vale it knew well. Mila lifted her backside off the bed, pushed down her underpants, and allowed the re-entry to happen unhindered, knowing full well the sproutling carried inside it the lives of countless terminated fetuses. She would be the mothership for all of them. In time, life filled her inner being, causing a whirl of blood and warmth, creation and energy, to flow through underground chambers and hidden cloisters. Vitality ran the length of her body with the force and effervescence of creation's first pulse in primal oceans, pushing out darkness and bringing light to her eyes.

Haunting

Matilda

Matilda Craddock sat under the apple tree in Uncle Tom's yard, waiting for her parents to take her home. The flesh-like tendril that extended from her right hand and trailed along the ground like a bizarre skipping rope twitched sporadically, as though it possessed obscure remnants of life. It was dusk. In the stillness that settled over the valley, Matilda stretched on the ground and looked through the bare branches at the sky. She cast her mind into the immensity and grappled with the stars that glistened and winked, like sentient eyes, and imagined they sent mysterious messages meant for her alone, though she could not fathom what they would say to an insignificant child. Her concentration was so intense that she almost forgot to listen to the hum of conversation coming from the house.

Her mother said, "It's late, Jervase. Let's get going."

"Righto, Juney," Matilda's father replied and scraped back his chair.

But Uncle Tom wasn't ready to release his guests yet. He said, "How about one for the road, eh?"

Matilda heard the edge of a bottle strike the lip of a glass, followed by the measured gurgle of liquor.

"You two are hopeless," June Craddock said. "It's a wonder you can still stand up."

The Craddock brothers cackled evilly.

"Where is she?" said June Craddock.

"Where's who?" said her husband.

"Your daughter," replied his wife.

"Dunno. Outside, probably."

The question broke Matilda's musings. She stood and smoothed her dress. The skipping rope tightened its grip on her wrist and fed its fleshy substance into the main artery until the entire length vanished in her arm. It wouldn't do to let her parents see. They would never understand. Matilda passed through the back door into the kitchen. Her uncle's house was a basic soldier settlement farm, sat in the middle of wattle and stringy bark scrub.

Matilda's father looked up from his glass and cried, "Here she is." He pulled his daughter close. "Sleepy?"

Matilda shook her head, more to clear the alcohol fumes that encircled the table than to answer the question.

Her mother said, "Jervase, let's go." She scooped up the playing cards strewn on the table and secured them with an elastic band. "We've got a long day tomorrow." She stood up and, out of habit, began to clear the table.

"Put on your cardie. It'll be chilly out," she said without looking at Matilda. She piled glasses and several plates in the sink. "Are you going be all right?" she said to her brother-in-law. "We can stay the night if you want." Though there was hesitancy in her voice.

"I'm fine," Tom Craddock replied, rising to his feet. "I'll have to get used to being on me own from here on."

June Craddock gave him a pat on the back as though she were burping a baby. "Come a little early tomorrow. Maybe around lunchtime, before they arrive."

Tom Craddock nodded, though he was none too sure about the prospect of the solitary life that loomed before him now his wife Primrose was gone.

Jervase Craddock pushed away from the table and stood. He swayed on his feet. "Juney, you get the hurricane lamp. I'll saddle up the horse."

June Craddock whirled round. "No, you don't. You're not fit to tie your shoelaces, let alone go near a horse. I don't want another death on my hands. I'll do it. You can light the lamp. The wick is new, and I filled it up earlier."

In a few short minutes June Craddock returned with a stringy chestnut mare. Jervase Craddock hoisted his daughter on the animal's back and told her to sit tight. The night was dark as a feather on a crow's back. The sky formed a bejeweled dome over the house and pressed on the land an infinity of stars, galaxies, Nebulae.

"You walk ahead with the lamp so we can see where we're going," June Craddock said, shoving her husband between the shoulder blades. "Make yourself useful."

Jervase Craddock faced his brother. "See ya tomorrow."

Tom Craddock nodded and leaned against the verandah post until his brother's family passed through the gate and entered the unfettered country beyond.

Home for Jervase Craddock and his family was almost three miles away. The dirt track nudged the edge of the forest. Although there was no wind, the she-oaks made ghost-like sibilant noises to the right. Matilda loved the sound in the day and often lay under the trees to listen to their talk, but she dreaded to think what secrets they exchanged at night, what plots they hatched behind her back. Astride the horse, she focused on the light that came from the lamp in her father's raised hand. Jervase Craddock was first in line; his wife followed close behind, holding on to the horse with its precious cargo.

Sometime later the path dipped down to a noisy creek.

Without turning her head, June Craddock said, "Don't fall off, Missy."

Matilda wedged the remains of her hands between the horn and rise in the saddle—not that she needed to; a slender flexible appendage emerged from both wrists to bind her to the seat, bolting her to the saddle. The horse couldn't throw her even if it took off.

The fingers and thumbs on Matilda's hands had been cleanly sheared off at the second knuckle. It happened so long ago that Matilda could not remember a time when she did not have the full use of her hands. Possibly she had been born like that—the way George Marshall's boy was born with twisted arms and legs.

The horse clattered across the creek. Soon after, the family emerged from the hollow onto the plain. Even so, the fireflies that lived beside the creek and filled the surface of the water with light refused to leave Matilda alone. They pranced round her head and spread to the lower branches of trees until the world was festooned with blinking lights. Matilda smiled and gazed in wonder.

The lamp in Jervase Craddock's hand threw light on a lone grave under a stout gum tree. A bunch of daisies wilted on the freshly dug mound. Matilda forgot about the fireflies and turned her attention to her aunt's final resting place. It was peculiar to think of Primrose Craddock under the earth. It did not make sense. So very deep under. The dry soil, filled with crawling things and trailing roots of plants. It's no place for a human being. The funeral, such as it was, had taken place that morning. Matilda had stood at the edge of the grave and looked down at the makeshift coffin and it seemed to her it was being cast in a hungry maw that could chew up her aunt and spit her out, clean of skin, gleaming with bone.

June Craddock sighed and stopped in her tracks. The horse with Matilda on its back came to a halt behind her.

"Stupid woman," she said, shaking her head. "Stupid, stupid woman."

When the news broke about Primrose Craddock's sudden demise, Uncle Tom told Matilda that his wife had gone to sleep and never woke up. This rare sign of sensitivity and consideration on the part of her uncle was misplaced. Matilda was no fool. She didn't believe him for a minute. There was no doubt in her mind there was a shattered body inside the rectangular box. It would never walk or talk again. Even so, Matilda hoped that Uncle Tom's melancholy wife had gone to a better place in the end.

June Craddock told her husband to wait and walked to her sister-in-law's grave. Her husband let off an exasperated sigh and, lifting the lamp higher, peered at his wife's back. June Craddock stood beside the grave, a strand of dark-brown hair streaming behind her in the breeze that sprang up and rushed through the treetops. The sound traveled from the topmost branches down to the wildflowers that sprout upon the ground. In no time at all, the world was filled with a malevolent hissing and thrashing of plant life.

Alarmed, Matilda wrapped her finger stumps round the tentacle that held her to the saddle. It congealed in her hand to the consistency and texture of wood and she used it to rap sharply against the saddle's hardened leather. For some reason, she wanted to warn her mother. All it did was frighten the horse. It threw back its head and whinnied.

After a respectful couple of minutes, June Craddock returned to her husband's side.

"Let's go."

"What was that about?" he asked.

"Paying my last respects, stupid cow that she was. I'll never understand it or forgive her for doing it."

They set off. The open valley fell behind. Trees closed in again, blocking the wind, hemming in the path that made a steady course for home.

"She's only got herself to blame," Jervase Craddock said after a lengthy silence. His big strong hand gleamed in the lamplight, the hair on his knuckles clearly defined.

"The point is," his wife uttered, "she was your brother's wife and my sister-in-law. It's right to mourn the dead."

"No one forced her to do herself in."

"She couldn't cope; didn't understand. That's all."

Her husband chuckled darkly, but with affection. "We're not all as tough as you, love."

"She just couldn't deal with what we do for a crust," June answered thickly. "I knew she wouldn't even try to understand when she found out. That's why I didn't want her to be involved."

"Yeah, but fancy throwing yourself off a cliff... Imagine finding that—"

June Craddock cast a wary eye on her daughter.

Matilda pretended to be absorbed in the fireflies that continued to swarm round her head, making her resemble the Queen of Heaven. She knew Aunt Primrose killed herself by jumping off the cliffs surrounding Starve Crow. It was a big fall too. Like leaping off the edge of the world.

"You know what her problem was?"

June Craddock didn't want to know, but she was sure her husband was going to tell her anyway.

"She was mad. She believed all that crap about things living in the hills. You and me, we dish that bulldust out for the sake of the disciples, but Prim believed it. She was off with the fairies." He drew on his cigarette. "Tom shouldn't have married her. Blacks are trouble. She wasn't all there, I tell you." He blew a plume of smoke in the air to punctuate his statement.

His wife backed him up. "Times are tough. You do what you have to do to survive."

"Where there's demand, there's supply."

"If we don't do it, someone else will." June hoped that was the end of the conversation.

But Jervase wasn't finished. "Didn't she know we're in the middle of a depression? The money we make out of our little business put food on her table as well as ours. Maybe she preferred to starve, or eat witchetty grubs?"

Husband and wife laughed, shook their heads as if some people are beyond understanding.

Several minutes passed before June Craddock said, "The irony is we wouldn't be doing any of this if it weren't for Prim. She knew about the altar and what it'd been used for. If it wasn't for her, you would have tossed it out with the rest of the garbage in the basement."

"True enough," her husband conceded. "That rock is the best prop we've got."

"Yep. No altar, no disciples. No disciples, no money," June said, rubbing her forefinger against her thumb.

Jervase Craddock snorted. "Disciples my foot. More like a bunch of perves."

"Ach," June Craddock uttered, "they haven't a shilling's worth of sense between them."

"You know why?"

"Nope."

"They think with their pricks and not their brains," Jervase hooted, giving her a kiss on the cheek.

"And that's fine with me," June said, linking her arm to his. "That's just fine with me."

Husband and wife pressed toward each other and continued to walk as though they were lovers taking a solitary stroll in the forest.

There were no houses along this stretch of road. Matilda knew that she and her parents were alone. Should anything happen, no one would have an inkling. The further they walked, the deeper the isolation. The night, the immense silence, closed in like a trap, surrounding the travelers until they and the flimsy bubble of light in which they walked appeared to float in space.

Matilda tensed up on the horse. She had a sense that something stood far back in the woods, watching. The realization tightened every muscle in her body. Her head turned to the left and then to the right, as though she were a bat using sonar to track down her quarry. She cast out her mind and, by degrees, became aware of the thing waiting farther back in the trees, pacing its movements with the light that bobbed on the road. She couldn't bear to look directly at it. She only sensed its presence and caught occasional glimpses as it flitted between tree trunks with astonishing speed. It was as though it flew or glided, long tendrils reaching out from the body to wrap round trees and pull it along, several feet above ground.

Matilda knew it waited for someone to step out of the light—for a moment. Then it would pounce.

"Gotta take a leak," Jervase Craddock said. He handed the lamp to his wife and wandered into the bush. He didn't hear the whine his daughter made in her throat, or if he did, he ignored it.

Matilda leaped off the horse and raced after him, wailing.

June Craddock placed the hurricane lamp on the ground and grabbed her.

"Wait on. Do you want to pee as well?"

Matilda shook her head and pointed at her father, eyes wide with fear.

June Craddock held on. "He'll be back in a sec. Calm yourself."

Matilda shook her head again and struggled in her mother's arms. June held on. Matilda flailed and kicked.

"What's the matter with you? Listen, he's taking a piss. He'll be ba—"

She didn't finish the sentence. The air was torn asunder by a horrific scream.

June Craddock had been married to Jervase for twelve years. They'd been through a lot together. She knew he was nowhere near as tough as he ought to be. But in all that time, she had never heard such exultant terror in his voice. She called his name and turned to dash after him. Matilda wrapped her arms round her mother's waist and held on with all her strength, shaking her head and making a rasping croak in her throat, eyes wide with alarm.

June Craddock yelled, "Let go," and pushed her daughter aside. Matilda fell but managed to wrap both her arms round her mother's left ankle. The screaming in the bush intensified to an unbearable pitch. The panic, the sheer fright of it barely sounded human. Birds clattered out of trees and there was a loathsome recoil in the air, as if the atmosphere was disturbed and vibrating to an unknown song.

June Craddock shouted again, "Let go," and delivered a sharp kick to Matilda's head with the heel of her boot. Matilda collapsed in the dust. June ran into the dark, calling her husband's name. In her haste she forgot the hurricane lantern.

Matilda rose to her feet and tried to hook the stumps of two fingers through the metal ring at the top of the lantern. It was in vain. There wasn't enough flesh and bone to grasp the ring. She almost wailed with frustration. As though sensing her helplessness, a fleshy hook slid from her left wrist and attached to the lamp. Matilda hurried after her mother, light tilting madly at her feet.

Jervase Craddock's screams had been replaced by a wet gurgling that reminded Matilda of an overflowing drain in a storm.

In all her years Matilda had not wanted to speak, never wanted to relate what she saw and thought to anyone. But she wished for a voice now. She wanted to call, "Stop Mom. Don't go. You're safe in the light. It's too late for Dad." Yet nothing came out except the lowing of a pathetic cow. She despised herself. She wished she were dead.

Matilda became aware that she couldn't see her mother. She wiped blood from her eyes and listened. Her forehead throbbed where her mother kicked her. She heard June's bulk push through the undergrowth to the right. Matilda raised the lantern and peered in the dark. Her mother was ahead, struggling through the undergrowth. From nearby came the sound of water pelting the ground in a torrent. It looked to Matilda as if her mother was running toward a waterfall. On second thoughts it didn't sound like water at all. It was too luxuriantly thick and creamy for that, full of spattering globules. Matilda heard her father make a final choked stammer, lavish with agony and torment. There came a terrible breaking sound, like a bundle of twigs snapping in two. The silence that fell was worse than the preceding noise.

June Craddock stood with her back to her daughter. A pale gum tree loomed in front of her and the light, as Matilda approached from behind, threw dancing shadows over the grisly scene. Jervase Craddock had been sliced in half at the waist. The chest was open, and blood covered the ground. The gore was a sleek, satiny black, a lustrous steaming alloy that coated rock and grass and tree in shimmering striations. Most surprising was a severed hand that gripped an impossibly high branch and dripped red in a viscous trail along the length of the tree trunk. And it seemed to Matilda that the ground, the very soil, lapped up her father's blood with insatiable lips.

Matilda stepped closer to her mother. She did not dare touch the woman. She did not dare breathe for fear of disturbing her. For the time being it was enough to keep her mother safe in the light.

June Craddock was a tough, practical woman, a roll-up-your-sleeves country type. She lived life with pig-headed determination and performed her tasks with fanatical commitment. Life was about survival, the business of getting from one day to the next without succumbing to hardship. There was nothing else. In all her years she never wavered from that singular mission. These qualities made her invaluable to the Craddock brothers and saw her triumph where others failed. She wasn't one to break up and cry that's for sure.

She faced her daughter. "Let's get out of here," she said. Her voice was final, steely. But she stumbled more than once in the scrub and leaned on Matilda for support.

When they joined the mare on the forest path June Craddock said, "Hold on a minute."

Matilda turned to her mother, blinking tears out of her eyes and doing her best not to wail.

"Do we go back to Tom's or do we keep going to our place?" June Craddock asked.

It was a sign of indecision Matilda had not seen before. Her mother was definitely rattled.

Matilda pointed the way ahead. It made sense to go home. At this stage they were closer to their own house than Uncle Tom's farm. It was safer, faster, to go home. In the morning, they'd come back to collect her father's body, if the animals didn't get to it first.

June Craddock glared at Matilda. And before Matilda could see it coming, June slapped her hard across the face. For the second time that night, Matilda fell to the ground. The hurricane lamp tumbled from her hand. The light guttered and went out. Blackness fell on the scene. June Craddock pounced on her daughter and grabbed her by the throat.

"You useless cunt," she cried. "This happened because of you. This is your fault. You know who did this, don't you? The bloke from Bendigo, that's who. He did this to Jervase. He wouldn't have done it if you'd let him screw you. He followed us and he killed my husband, just like he said he would. It's your fault. You killed my mate...the only thing I..." June's voice broke. "You took him from me." She raved and squeezed, bashing Matilda's head to the ground. "But oh no you were too sore. What good are you? Whore. Can't even do that properly."

Matilda didn't fight back. Her mother was right. It was her fault. She was to blame. She should have let the man from Bendigo put his thing in her during last month's ceremony.

Matilda remembered the disastrous gathering. Rituals were held the first Thursday of the month in the basement of her house, well away from prying eyes. Worshipers gathered from three o'clock onwards. They encircled the altar and stood naked beneath their long gray robes until her father lit candles and performed a cleansing ceremony. It was meant to appease the "Sleepers in the Hills" before the disciples got down to the business of purifying their bodies for the coming resurrection. On that particular day, however, they'd been interrupted. For some reason, Aunt Primrose came to the house and discovered what went on in the underground room. She went berserk when she saw a man on top of Matilda. She screamed and pummeled him, until her husband Tom hit her in the face and told her to shut up. That quieted her, but she refused to let them continue with "this blasphemy," as she put it, "this evil." Through tears, she declared her disgust with what was going on, the ugly usage of a child. To make matters worse, it happened in front of the gathering. That was very silly of her. Uncle Tom hadn't wasted a moment. He dragged his wife upstairs and "kicked the shit out of her," as he later told his brother and sister-in-law over a beer.

Matilda heard the assault take place upstairs as she lay on the stone altar in the basement. She had been so upset that, try as she might, she couldn't play her usual part in the ceremony. She was very sore after the second man. And four more waited their turn. Even so, Matilda tried not to complain. She knew the family relied on her to make money, and that the men who traveled from all over the state to possess for a few vital minutes a precious miracle, which, they claimed, prepared their weak flesh for the day when "the Sleepers" stepped forth from the portal between her legs. Nevertheless, Matilda cried out and turned away her face when the third man—the one from Bendigo—climbed atop her. He had been angered by the girl's behavior. He claimed it was an insult to the gods and showed disrespect for the ritual. He wanted his money back or else. Jervase Craddock refused. "Once money exchanges hands, mate, that's it," he said. "Now bugger off, the lot o'ya. She's crook."

All the same, the man who didn't get his money's worth had been furious. He'd come a long way, he said, and now he was supposed to go without being purified? No way. He'd get his own back, he threatened. Just you wait and see...

But Matilda knew that the disgruntled disciple from Bendigo did not kill her father. It was the thing in the forest.

By now Matilda's face was blue. Her green eyes bulged from the sockets; eyes she kept shut while grown men pressed her skin, and while Mom and Dad collected cash from the punters. Matilda's tongue protruded from her mouth. She gasped for air, clawed the dirt. Her mother's enraged face loomed over her. The hard, calloused hands clasped the tender throat. The fingers squeezed tight as she throttled the life out of the "cash cow," as Uncle Tom laughingly called his niece.

"Are you a cash cow, Matilda? Are you our cash cow, little girl? Come over here and give us a kiss. There you go. Don't go growing up too fast. We need you. Aunty Prim can't have a baby to replace you. Her womb is barren as the Nullabor."

Matilda nodded and smiled and did as she was told. She loved her mom and dad. She adored her uncle and aunt. She put all her trust in them. They looked after her and she wanted to do right by them. Always. And so, the men congregated every month in the basement.

Matilda's eyes rolled back in her head. Only the whites were visible. Spittle dribbled from her mouth. It felt as if her body belonged to someone else. By the minute she was weightless and far away. Floating. Outside her body. Outside the world. It was nice. No fear. No pain. And it didn't hurt so much, this not being able to breathe. Her lungs bursting, throat bulging. And still her mother squeezed. Saliva and tears dripped from her onto Matilda's face.

Matilda's breath came in harsh gasps. Her fingers loosened and the skipping rope slipped out of her wrist. No one noticed when it slithered snake-like away from the mortal combat of mother and daughter. Then everything changed. June Craddock gasped and her grip on Matilda's throat relaxed. She jerked violently back and away from her daughter's prone body, falling hard on her backside.

Matilda sat up, coughing and retching, her head spinning. She opened her eyes and saw the skipping rope coil swiftly several times round her mother's neck. Nothing and no one held it. It had life of its own. Then, with an appalling shriek, her mother's body was hoisted up into the sky. Matilda saw June's dark outline, like a cutout doll, rise up against a background of stars. Higher and higher in the firmament she went, until it seemed she was a witch in flight. It was almost beautiful to see. When the body stopped the upward ascent, Matilda saw that it hung by the neck from the highest branch in a tree, feet kicking pitiably. Matilda gasped. A pall spread from her mother's body to obscure the stars, the moon, and the sky. It resembled a storm cloud in February. Then it swarmed down and engulfed her.

*

When sense returned, Matilda lay at the base of the stairs in her house. Sunlight flooded the grimy windows. Unearthly quiet ruled the world. She sat up and rubbed her eyes. It had been a bad dream. Yes, she would go upstairs and check on her mom and dad. No doubt they were in bed, asleep. She would scrounge together breakfast in the kitchen and take it upstairs for them to enjoy. But why was the front door open and why was she on the floor? A sound caught her attention: footsteps on the floor above.

Here comes Mom, Matilda thought. *She'll know what's going on.*

Matilda turned and knew from the gasp that escaped her throat it had not been a nightmare. It had been real, and it was not over.

Aunt Primrose stood at the top of the stairs.

Had he been present, Tom Craddock would not recognize his wife in her current state. In life Primrose Craddock had been a paltry figure, insubstantial, inconsequential. She had been plain, easily forgotten. Death had transformed her almost beyond recognition. Like a sculptor working on putrescent flesh, the Dark Angel had wrought a creation from beyond the stars, a soaring elongated column of radiant pitch. Had she been carved from darkest obsidian Primrose could not have been more beautiful, more bewitching, and more terrifying. Her allure as she stood at the top of the stairs, staring down at her niece, was devastating. She drew the eye and repelled it simultaneously. She was a mirror whose radiance possessed a moon-like coldness. It sucked in light and rejected warmth. She was utterly alien. As she came down the stairs, everything melted round her. The house vanished. The wooden steps and banister were gone. Matilda held her breath. She stood in outer space as her aunt drew closer and closer, sparkling and crackling as unseen particles struck her skin. Where the long hair ought to be, Matilda noticed, was a series of twitching, twisting feelers, stiff tactile barbs, and sensory organs with pulpy mouths and suckers. The woman had no legs. She slithered. Half a dozen elongated appendages covered her lower half and propelled her forward in rapid flowing movements.

Matilda had liked her aunt's inelegance; there was something safe and comforting about it. Before this disquieting vision she was humbled, shy, uncertain. She rose to her feet and stared with reverence. That's when she noticed that the entity (for she could no longer think of the stellar being as homely Aunt Primrose) was carrying something.

A glass jar rested in the palm of each hand and, as the creature approached, liquid moved thickly inside the containers. One jar appeared to contain pale asparagus spears and the other chunky pink fruit.

Primrose stood in front of her niece. She smiled and in that instant outer space vanished. The room reappeared as if it were a curtain drawn across a stage to block out the vast cosmos. Reality snapped back in place, exactly as it had been. The creature placed the jars on a small occasional table by the staircase.

"My little love," she said, bending down and placing an ice-cold finger on Matilda's begrimed lips. "Your salvation is at hand. Everything will be all right." Neither male nor female, the voice had two tones: a bass and a treble that melded and clashed, weaving in and out of each other to create uncanny music.

Primrose dipped her hand in one jar and placed the peculiar pink fruit in her mouth. Then she leaned forward and kissed Matilda on the forehead. Matilda closed her eyes and breathed in the earthy aroma that came from the thing's skin. Lips moved from Matilda's forehead to the bridge of her nose. There to linger briefly before sealing Matilda's lips with a firm kiss.

In her life Matilda had known many a grizzled kiss from hoary men. None had been as tender and passionate as this. She opened her own mouth and allowed the creature's tongue to enter and probe. A rigid insistent object pushed into Matilda's mouth. She choked, spluttered, attempted to cry out, tried to withdraw, but the thing had locked its mouth to Matilda's so that they were welded to one another. Feelers, tentacles, and claws kept the child in place. Matilda fought to free herself, eyes wide, beating the thing on the shoulders; muffled cries escaping from round their bonded lips. She became aware of a paralyzing coldness in her mouth, and when Primrose pulled back and stood smiling icily, Matilda cried out.

"Stop, stop. You're hurting me."

She stared. Who had spoken? Surely that had not been her. Yet the words had emerged from behind her teeth. A tongue that had not been there previously moved inside the cavity in her head.

"Who said that?"

"You did."

"Me?"

"You, my little love."

Matilda waggled the tongue inside her mouth. It was too big, too awkward and invasive. Yet it allowed her to produce words for the first time in memory.

Wonderstruck, she said, "I've grown a tongue."

"Until last night it belonged to Jervase Craddock. Since he saw fit to cut out your tongue, the least he can do is allow you the use of his. He won't need it anymore," Primrose added when she saw the look of horror on Matilda's face.

Primrose gave one of her gelid smiles and picked up the other jar from the table. "Sit. It's time to restore the fingers that were so cruelly taken from you."

Matilda sat on the second stair. Extending a tentacle, Primrose pulled over a chair and sat opposite her niece in the oblong of sunlight streaming through the open door. She produced thread and needle and, one by one, proceeded to sew the ten fingers that floated inside the second jar to the end of Matilda's hands.

Matilda recognized her mother's gold wedding ring on one finger and the scar on the left forefinger where June Craddock accidentally cut herself with a knife not six weeks ago.

Like the tongue in her mouth, the fingers were too big for Matilda's hand. They were wrong. But it didn't matter. No sooner did the creature finish sewing one finger to Matilda's hand then it began to move of its own accord, like an octopus eager for something to clutch.

The seamstress spoke as she worked.

"Once upon a time, there was a little girl. Her name was Matilda. She was the prettiest, most darling child in the world. Everyone admired her green eyes and flaxen hair. But no more so than her parents, Jervase and June Craddock.

"Jervase Craddock and his brother Tom came to this valley after the Great War. The government had given Tom Craddock a soldier settlement, but there was no such kindness for the cowardly older brother. Jervase had spent most of the war years hiding in the mountains. When Jervase Craddock and his wife June decided to squat in this house," Primrose's eyes roamed ceiling, walls, floor, "it had been empty for a long time.

"Soon after, a gorgeous little girl was bestowed upon the couple. As she grew older, stories about her uncanny beauty spread. People went out of their way to stop at the porch and admire her. They said her loveliness was beyond belief, haunting.

"One day, while clearing the basement, Jervase Craddock chanced upon a peculiar object—a large white rock, covered with mysterious hieroglyphs. Jervase didn't know it, of course," Primrose said, "but this was the heart of the great and winding snake. He fell to earth in the beginning time. His body shattered. The sun bleached his heart and turned it to white rock with his story written on it in a language no one could speak or understand. The great snake is the creator of all there is to see. He is the end of all seeking. Break the code of the stone and you open a doorway for him and all the others like him to return."

Primrose revealed stories of a secret cult that existed many years earlier. "White men all—a good dozen—who still lived hereabouts until a few years ago," she added to her rapt audience. "A man called Walter Whiteley found the altar. He bought the land and built a house atop it. On certain nights he and the disciples went down the basement to talk to the Ancients. But it was a sick, twisted calling. They were playing with fire and did not know it."

The story thrilled Matilda. So much was making sense. So many little questions were being answered. It was funny and scary at the same time.

"Primrose, the former owner of this body, told Jervase and June about the stone. Once they discovered its secret history, they had their pretext. What they'd been looking for all along. They could now open for business.

"The husband put out the word. First came one and then another. At first curious and cautious and only after dark, when the moon had set and shadow lay thick upon the ground, and then in a more daring fashion, during the day. They all came with money. They all craved one thing: to see the famed altar and to possess upon its surface the child with green eyes."

Matilda tilted her head.

"Did the altar make them?"

Primrose looked up with a smile.

"Not entirely. Some things lie deep inside a man's heart. So deep and buried that even he may not know it exists. All it takes is for one small thing to bring it to the surface and he will give it free rein." Primrose removed a finger from the jar and continued.

"Word spread. The defilement upon the girl's body continued. One day Matilda's mother said, 'She's getting older. The law might hear of it. We're done for if she talks. Cut out her tongue.'

"And so, Jervase cut out Matilda's tongue with a pair of shears from the barn. It was a miracle she did not die. Business went on as usual. A year or so later the mother said, 'She can't talk, but she can write. What if she writes a note? Chop off her fingers.'

"Jervase held Matilda down while her mother put the little hand on the chopping block and chop-chopped off her fingers with a hatchet. Finally, they had the perfect moneymaker. The girl couldn't talk and she couldn't write, but she could be of service.

"The father convinced his brother Tom to get in on the act. It didn't take much to convince him. He's a bad lot, in some ways worse than his older brother."

Primrose stopped, reached in the jar, removed another finger, and continued the tale.

"Tom Craddock's wife, Primrose, did not know what went on in the basement, but she had her suspicions. That's why they kept her away and she was not involved."

Ah, Matilda thought, *now we're coming to the interesting bit.* Her entire being tingled with excitement.

"Do you know who the Elder Things are?" Primrose asked.

Matilda almost shook her head. Then, remembering her new voice, said, "No."

When the creature spoke again it sounded as if several different voices came out of its mouth. "We are the foregone conclusion, whisperers in the Dark Bower. Older than the earth that harbors us in water, air, and rock, we are supreme, all-encompassing. We are shredders of reality. The eagle on the wing. The cat on the prowl. The breath in the fossil. We live inside hills and wait..."

Next came a crystal note, an utterly feminine voice: "Did you know that Walter Whiteley succeeded in opening the door to the Elder Things?"

Matilda was content to merely shake her head.

"Indeed he did. And do you know what else, my little love?" The thing that was less and less like Primrose Craddock every minute rubbed noses with Matilda.

Delighted, Matilda giggled.

"What?"

"You are not your father's daughter." Primrose laughed and clapped her hands, delighted, as if she had told the funniest joke at someone else's expense. "Jervase

Craddock had nothing to do with you. His seed was infertile. The Wordless Voice—He who was born without a father—seeded June Craddock. In the throes of passion, the god slipped between Jervase and June and beget himself a daughter fair..."

"Oh," Matilda said, finally catching on.

Primrose was down to two fingers. The thread and needle passed in and out of Matilda's skin, painlessly stitching June Craddock's hard-working fingers to Matilda's undersized hand, one by one; *snick-snick* went the scissors on the black thread. When the manicurist finished, she leaned back and admired her handiwork.

"Beautiful," she said. "You are complete. Now you can go into the world a picture of loveliness. Remember two things. Always wear black gloves. And never forget that the tongue and fingers will last the passage of one full moon. Then they will go the way of all flesh and must be replaced with a fresh tongue and fresh fingers. Do you understand?"

"Yes," Matilda replied, delighting in the word. "Yes, I do."

This time there was real warmth in Primrose's smile.

"When the disciples gather this afternoon," she said, "don't kill them all at once. Imprison them in the basement and take them one by one at your will. Then you will be sure to have a ready supply of tongues and fingers in the pantry. Keep the spare ones in this solution." She tapped a jar.

"Will do."

Primrose returned her niece's smile. "Time to get ready for Uncle Tom," she said. "He will soon be here, my little love."

*

What a dump, Tom Craddock thought. What a disgrace.

He spat his disgust at the dry grass. It was high noon. He stood outside his brother's house and shook his head. How had the best house in Starve Crow become the district's biggest eyesore?

The old Whiteley house, a run-down Victorian gothic revival erected at the end of the nineteenth century, had been empty for well on a decade. It wasn't big but it was smart. A weatherboard and brick confection, it boasted two floors and shady verandahs front and back. Locals called it the Crooked House, for the simple reason that the edifice was sinking into the ground; or, more accurately, into the basement. The descent caused bricks to split, wood to warp and the house to tilt wildly to one side, so that looking at it was a matter of leaning your head to the left and adjusting your vision to suit the skewed perspective. It gave the place an awry feel, as if things weren't right with the world.

As Tom stepped on the front porch, he noted that the shutters over the windows were closed. So was the usually open front door. The total absence of sound struck him. Nothing. Not even his sister-in-law's wireless, or the scratching of chickens. It made him uneasy. Still it was nothing compared to the god-awful silence he endured in the marital bed last night. He didn't want to go through that again. For all her faults, his wife Primrose had been a warm, reassuring presence. He'd grown used to her.

He knocked on the begrimed glass set in the front door and, as was his habit, walked in without waiting for an answer. He passed from room to room. Saw no one.

"Hello," he called. "Anyone here?" His voice echoed in the empty house.

"Down here." The husky male voice sounded like his brother Jervase.

Tom Craddock came down the stairs, ducked at the last minute to avoid a low beam, and entered the basement.

Matilda was alone. Dressed in a handsome black dress, she sat primly on the altar, feet dangling, hands clasped delicately in her lap. A flickering candle lit the gloomy scene. June and Jervase were nowhere in sight.

"Where's your mom and dad?"

He expected no reply.

"Are they out?"

Matilda smiled and looked at him from under her eyelashes.

A grin spread on Tom's face. *Hel-lo,* he thought. *The slut wants me.*

He always knew—hoped—it would come to this.

He walked up to his niece and stood over her, looked in her eyes, bit his lip. Then he kneeled and brought his face to her eye level.

"Got something for Uncle Tom?" he said deliberately.

Matilda nodded. Then, with one swift movement, she lifted her skirt and displayed her prize.

Tom sucked in a breath, placed his hands on her knees, and leaned forward.

"What have we here...?"

An eye opened between the girl's legs and stared at him. Tom Craddock managed a "What the fuck?" before a frenzy of tentacles leaped out of Matilda's groin and attached to his face. His screams were muffled by the appendages that swarmed in his mouth and poured down his throat. A flexible limb tightened at his throat and with the tumultuous wriggling of a squid more waxen limbs streamed up his nostrils and into his ears. He was lifted bodily from the ground. As he rose into the air, he looked at his niece's face and saw that the attributes of a normal face had been obliterated. In their place flitted the features of his wife and then his niece; his brother and his sister-in-law featured in rapid succession. The faces shot by like images in a flick book, overlapped, merged, formed, reformed, and inexorably slowed until Matilda's face coalesced into a semblance of itself. Only now she possessed four mouths in descending order, from forehead to chin. All were lined with sharp, evil-looking teeth. Then a tentacle scooped out Tom Craddock's eyeballs and squirmed into the empty sockets. In the darkness that fell he heard his dearly departed wife say, "Be careful with his tongue, my little love."

Acknowledgements

The Long Lonely Road, first published in the online magazine, *Zin Daily*, Liznjan, Croatia, 2017. *The Boy by the Gate*, first published in *The New Gothic,* Stone Skin Press, London, England, 2013, and reprinted in *Best Australian Fantasy and Horror 2013,* Ticonderoga Publications, Greenwood, Western Australia, 2014. *Haunting Matilda*, first published in *Cthulhu Deep Down Under*, Horror Australis, Melbourne, Australia, 2015.

A short essay on how *The Door* came to be written can be found at:

www.thedrunkenodyssey.com/2017/02/20/pensive-prowler-4-how-not-to-write-a-short-story

About the Author

Dmetri Kakmi was born in Turkey to Greek parents. His fictionalized memoir *Mother Land* was shortlisted for the New South Wales Premier's Literary Awards in Australia; and is published in England and Turkey. Dmetri also edited the acclaimed children's anthology *When We Were Young*. His essays and short stories appear in anthologies. He lives in Melbourne, Australia.

Email: dmetrik443@gmail.com

Instagram: www.instagram.com/dmetrikakmi

Website: www.dmetrikakmi.com.au

Also Available from NineStar Press

Connect with NineStar Press

www.ninestarpress.com

www.facebook.com/ninestarpress

www.facebook.com/groups/NineStarNiche

www.twitter.com/ninestarpress